THE MISSING GIRL

by

Norma Fox Mazer

HARPER TEEN

An Imprint of HarperCollins*Publishers*

HarperTeen is an imprint of HarperCollins Publishers.

The Missing Girl
Copyright © 2008 by Norma Fox Mazer
We gratefully acknowledge permission to reprint "postcard from cape cod." Copyright
© 1978, 1998 by Linda Pastan, from CARNIVAL EVENING: *New and Selected Poems
1968–1998* by Linda Pastan. Used by permission of W. W. Norton & Company, Inc.

Library of Congress Cataloging-in-Publication Data
Mazer, Norma Fox, 1931–
   The missing girl / by Norma Fox Mazer. — 1st ed.
      p. cm.
   Summary: In Mallory, New York, as five sisters, aged eleven to seventeen, deal
with assorted problems, conflicts, fears, and yearnings, a mysterious middle-aged
man watches them, fascinated, deciding which one he likes the best.
   ISBN 978-0-06-623776-3 (trade bdg.) — ISBN 978-0-06-623777-0 (lib.
bdg.)
   [1. Sisters—Fiction. 2. Family life—New York (State)—Fiction.
3. Kidnapping—Fiction. 4. Child sexual abuse—Fiction. 5. New York
(State)—Fiction.] I. Title.
PZ7.M47398Mig 2008   2007009136
[Fic]—dc22   CIP
                                                                      AC

Typography by Larissa Lawrynenko
1 2 3 4 5 6 7 8 9 10

First Edition

PART
ONE
WHO THEY ARE
AND HOW IT HAPPENS

A FLOCK OF BIRDS

IF THE MAN IS LUCKY, in the morning on his way to work, he sees the girls. A flock of them, like birds. March is a dismal month, and the man's spirits often fall during this month of wet clouds and short gray days. He is hard put to remember that soon spring will return, but the sight of a cardinal or a chickadee—or the girls—reminds him of this. He is not one of those strange people who watch birds through binoculars, but the twittering and calls of even the jays, who are abominably noisy, is refreshing to him. As is the twittering and chatter of the girls.

One, two, three, four, five. Five of them. *Five*. A gratifying outcome of changing his route to work. Without being unduly self-congratulatory, because he is a modest man, he can take credit for this, as a result of his intelligence and careful planning. When his job description changed, he knew immediately that this meant he should no longer walk the same streets from his house to the bus stop to the store office. And though the route he had used for the past year was decidedly efficient, he changed it, proving once again that he was—he *is*—highly adaptable. It is the adaptable who survive in this beastly world.

It takes him seven minutes longer to walk the new way, but if one thing changes, then something else must change as well. This is a rule, the only way to maintain balance and order. The proof of the fundamental rightness of this rule is clear: changing the streets he walks to the bus stop each morning brought the girls into his life. An unexpected gift.

A reward, because he has been good for so long.

He has always liked schoolgirls, their open faces, their laughter, their innocence. Despite the fact that he has now seen these particular girls, his flock of birds, nearly a dozen times, not one of them has noticed him. Not one of them has flicked him so much as a glance. This is good. It's the way he wants it. He doesn't want to be noticed. It is safer to be, as he knows he is, unremarkable.

Slight of build, stoop shouldered, wearing a gray coat, a gray scarf around his neck against the cold, his wire-rimmed glasses set firmly on his nose, minding his own business, he could be any man, any respectable, ordinary man.

LE PLAN

BEAUTY HERBERT, HURRYING down the hill from Mallory Central School, sliding a little on the slushy sidewalk, considered her age. Today, the snowy fifth of March, she was exactly seventeen and one-half years. The time for *Le Plan* was coming ever closer. Maybe she'd tell Patrick it was her half-year birthday, and he'd insist that they have a latte from the coffee shop across the street to celebrate.

Patrick Jimenez owned Patrick the Florist, the shop on Costello Street where Beauty worked ten hours a week and where she was headed now. *Seventeen and a half!* enthusiastic Patrick would say. *Great!* The latte, and then work. Patrick had been in the flower business for twenty-five years, and his customers adored him. Beauty did, too, as though he were not only her boss, but almost an older brother, the brother she'd always wished for to share the responsibility that came with being the oldest of five sisters.

The idea of leaving her little sisters, in fact, was the only thing about *Le Plan* that bothered Beauty. She wasn't too worried about Mim, who, at sixteen, seemed to be okay, but the newly fourteen-year-old sister who had just informed the family that she was changing her name from Faithful to *Stevie*, of all things, was something of a mess, drenching everyone in her out-there, high-speed, top-volume emotions and orders (*from now on, my name is Stevie and no one in this family better forget that*). As for Fancy and Autumn, well, they were both still kids, and that was the trouble. Who would look after them when she left? Fancy was twelve, had her period and little breasts, and should be growing up, but of course she wasn't. And eleven-year-old Autumn? Half the time the child was dreaming about something or other, and the other half crying over nothing. It didn't look as if she would ever make a plan for her life, as Beauty had done, but at least when she was here, Beauty could keep an eye on her.

Last September, when she had turned seventeen and also entered her senior year in high school, Beauty had rejoiced, as she was rejoicing today. Like mile markers on a highway, each month brought her that much closer to her eighteenth birthday, to the moment when *Le Plan* could become reality, when she was a legal adult, legally responsible for herself, legally able to do whatever she wanted—no, *needed*—to do.

Anyway, seventeen was, really, *so* much better than sixteen, which had been *so* much better than fifteen, which had been *so* much better than fourteen, which had been mostly a relief from the pain of thirteen. If there were a pill she could pop, like an aspirin, that would blot out thirteen and cruel seventh-grade humor, she would take it in a heartbeat. Although, she amended, crossing French Street against the light (sorry, Mom), she wouldn't want to forget Mr. Giametti. So, okay, the magic little pill could scrub her memory clean of a certain drawing, a certain poem, and leave in the good stuff.

Passing Lawler's department store on River Street downtown, she caught a glimpse of herself in the window and quickly looked away. She'd hatched *Le Plan* when she was thirteen, and she'd been carrying it around all these years. By next March on this date, she'd be long gone. She'd have a place of her own, a new life, a new job, and a new name (although not a ridiculous one like Stevie). *Le Plan!* Like the two words, the plan was neat and simple. It was just this: as soon as she turned eighteen, she was getting out of Dodge.

Dodge, in this case, was Mallory, this town of 5,329 people in northern New York State, where Beauty had lived her whole life. When she left Mallory, it would be for Chicago, which she had first heard about from Mr. Giametti, her seventh-grade language arts teacher, who grew up there. She was going to a place where no one knew her, a place where she could become whoever it was she was meant to be, whoever it was that she could never be in Mallory, where everyone had a tag, a label, a stifling little box into which they were shoved and where they were expected to stay forever.

The label on her little box? That ugly Herbert girl, poor thing, with the so-wrong name.

BELLYACHING

WHAT DO YOU DO when you don't want to go
to school? If you're Autumn and you're eleven, *only*
eleven, as you think of it, and the baby of the family, you
shuffle into the kitchen, train your eyes on your oldest sister, and say, with just a little whine in your voice, "Beauty.
Beauty. I have a bellyache." You hope you look sick. You
sniffle up the night junk in your nose and let your mouth
fall open a little.

You try to ignore Fancy, who says in her loud, eager
voice that she'll save the funnies for you. "I'm reading
them all by myself this morning," she says. You try not to
watch as she takes too big a gulp of milk, burps, and sets

the glass down with a thud to announce, "Uh-oh! Your feet are bare. Uh-oh! Autumn alarm! Autumn alarm!"

You pay attention to Beauty, who's looking at you now and pointing out the obvious, that you're still in your pajamas, that you're not dressed for school. "Get a move on," she says. You watch as she pours coffee into Mommy's cup, the one that says, "I ♥ MY MOM," and slides it over next to Mommy's ashtray.

You clutch your belly. "I have a stomachache," you repeat plaintively. And you add, "It hurts, it hurts," and as you say this, your belly really does hurt.

You look gratefully at your sister Mim, who says, "How bad is it, honey?"

"Bad," you say pitifully, and you think how much you love Mim, love how everything about her is *less*, unlike the rest of them. You love how small she is, how neatly made, and you love how her voice is so quiet. And you think, not for the first time, how you wish you were like Mim and everybody listened when you talked.

Then Beauty is asking if you're starting your period, maybe, and you shake your head. You know about periods and pads and blood and all that stuff that Mommy calls "the womanhood department." And you don't want to get sidetracked, so you bend over, clutching yourself, and you say the truth. "I don't want to go to school, okay?"

But Beauty shakes her head and says you have to ask Mommy, which is really annoying, since Beauty is the one who always writes the excuses. Then you watch as she sits down, picks up her own coffee cup, and reaches for a piece of the newspaper.

You stand there, clutching your belly, but now none of your sisters is paying any attention to you. They're all busy reading different parts of the newspaper, and you know what they're doing—searching for good stories to tell Mommy later on. Because Mommy always says, "Personally, I do not get this newspaper thing. Shit, I'm not going to read all the bad news. Don't do me any good. I got enough bad news of my own."

You think how you love stories, love making them up and hearing them and reading them, and Mommy does, too. She loves true stories, like she can get on TV, and she loves to listen to anyone telling her a good juicy story they've read in the newspaper, like that man who chopped up his wife and kept all her parts in a trunk in the attic for years? Well, actually, you don't like stories like that. They scare you.

After a while you shuffle out of the kitchen and up the stairs, thinking how nothing is fair in this family, how Fancy is spoiled, how Beauty gets to boss them all around, how Faithful—oops, *Stevie*—scares everyone with her temper, and Mim is so quiet she can do whatever she wants and nobody notices. You're the only one who has nothing special about you.

"It hurts, it hurts," you moan. You bump your head against the door of your parents' bedroom, and you say, "Mommy, I have to tell you something." Then you go in, and Mommy is standing in front of the mirror in her underwear, combing her hair, getting ready for work. She's a lunch lady at that home for old people downtown that used to be a church. You tell her about your stomach, and she puts her hand against your forehead, then presses on either side of your neck.

"It's my stomach," you remind her.

She says, "No fever. No swollen glands. What's happening in school today?" And she taps you a little bit hard on top of your head, which makes you want to cry.

You say, "Oral report. We have to tell a story about our family."

You can always make up stories for yourself and for

11

Fancy, but the oral report story has to be *true*. What are you supposed to say—that Mommy is fat and smokes too much and worries too much? That Poppy fell off a roof and hurt his back and can't do his regular work and is *so* grumpy? That Mommy and Poppy are mad at each other because of no work and no money?

"It's part of our social studies unit," you tell her.

And right away you're sorry you said it, because Mommy frowns and says in a mad voice, "Our family is part of your social studies unit? That's what we pay taxes for? So people can snoop on our family?"

You tell her it's an activity in the unit on The Family in America, and everyone has to do it. And in case she forgot, you add, in your most pitiful voice, "My stomach hurts."

Mommy bends, looking into your face, and says, "You don't have a stomachache."

"I do," you say, "I really do." You try not to smell Mommy's stale cigarette breath. You say, "When are you going to stop smoking?" and you take a step back. You remind her that you learned in your civics unit that smoking isn't healthy, and she should stop.

Which makes Mommy say, "You can be a regular pain in the butt." Which she says all the time to Stevie and

12

sometimes even to Beauty, so you don't mind too much. "And," she says, "I will never see what ciggies have to do with civics." So you tell her about the tobacco companies, and how they lied about cigarettes and the poison chemicals in them. And then Mommy says, as if she's never heard this before, "They lied?" And you tell her yes, and it was in all the newspapers and on the radio and TV.

"Maybe I forgot," she says. She's pulling a sweatshirt over her head. It gets stuck, but she's still talking. "Maybe I don't want to remember. I love my ciggies, and I know I overdo them, but what can I do? I have to have my ciggies."

Her head pops out, and she laughs a big hoarse laugh, which makes you smell her cigarette breath again. So you sit down on the edge of the bed and check the time. It's late, way too late to even think about going to school and oral reports.

Then Mommy says, "How's that stomach now?" and you say it hurts and you put your hands over your belly again.

Mommy goes from laughing to coughing, and her face gets all red and sweaty. When she can speak again, she says, "That's from overdoing the ciggies. Don't be like me, don't start with the habit. Once you start, you can't stop yourself."

You tell her she always says that. You say, "I am not going to smoke. And you should stop. Just make up your mind and do it." You like how you said that. Nice and firm.

"Little Miss Dictator," Mommy says, but she's smiling. You know you're her favorite, because you're the baby of the family, though you wouldn't have been if your little twin sisters had lived. But they hadn't, and you are.

"Oof," Mommy says, buttoning her jeans over her fat stomach. She sits down next to you on the bed to pull on socks and sneakers. She stands up with a little groan, looks at herself in the mirror, pushes her hands through her hair, and lights another cigarette.

"So, can I go back to bed now?" you ask. Downstairs the door slams, which means your sisters are going off to school. "I could rest in your bed," you suggest, and you're careful not to look at the TV, but only at Mommy, who's taking her hairnet for work out of the top drawer.

"You're going to school," Mommy says.

You're so surprised by this, you yelp, "Mommy!"

"Your stomachache ain't that bad," Mommy says. "I can tell."

And even though you know you shouldn't, you start arguing. "Where's Poppy? Poppy would let me stay home.

14

He understands more than you. Mommy, it's not fair."

"Never mind that stuff," Mommy says, and her voice tells you she means business. "Your father's sitting out in his truck, thinking things over, and he don't want to hear from you." She puts her hands on your shoulders and walks you out of her room and over to yours, the room you share with Fancy and Stevie. "Get dressed, you're going to school," Mommy says. "You're not missing school for no reason. You're going to stay with it and graduate, not like me."

You try to tell her you don't have to think about graduation stuff for a long time, you're only in fifth grade, but she doesn't want to listen. "Hurry up and get dressed," she says. She doesn't care that you'll have to run all the way to school, and you'll probably still be late.

That's the bad part.

The good part is that on the way to school—running, stopping to catch your breath, running again—you think of something you can say for your oral report. You can tell about Great-great-grandfather Ephraim Herbert, who came to Mallory from Ireland one hundred years ago. Or was it one hundred and eight? Well, whatever. Just say one hundred years, a *century*, and Mr. Spiegleman will think it's fantastic. He loves to hear about old times and old people and, well, anything old.

You won't repeat, though, the other stuff Poppy told you with that funny look on his face. Like he wanted to laugh, but he didn't think he should? Poppy always gets that look when he's about to tell Mommy a story that will make her say, "Huddle Herbert! Don't say them things in front of your girls."

Great-great-grandpa Ephraim had been an outlaw, which meant he was a *criminal*, a bad guy. Not that he ever hurt anybody—you would hate to know that about someone related to you—but he brewed bootleg whiskey in the woods, and once somebody shot him and he lived the rest of his life limping with a bullet in his leg.

"Do you know what Ephraim looked like, Autumn?" Mr. Spiegleman asks when you're done with your report in front of the class. "Do you have any family pictures?"

You shake your head and look up at the ceiling. It's hard for you to keep looking straight at Mr. Spiegleman. He's so cute with his long ponytail.

"No family stories about Ephraim?" Mr. Spiegleman says, almost as if he knows that you're holding out, and for a moment, glancing at him, your face gets *so* hot, and you

16

really want to tell him everything. But you don't, because, like Mommy says, family business is family business and nobody else's.

Later, at the end of the day, Mr. Spiegleman reminds you not to forget your excuse for being late. You say, "Don't worry, I won't."

"I'm not worrying about you, Autumn," he says, and he gives you a big smile, like maybe you're *his* favorite, too.

That evening Beauty writes the excuse for you. Mommy has Beauty take care of all that sort of stuff; she doesn't want to be bothered. Besides, Beauty has beautiful handwriting. Everybody says so.

Mr. Spiegleman:
Please excuse my daughter Autumn Herbert
for coming late to school Thursday morning. She
did not feel well when she woke up but recovered
sufficiently to attend her classes.
Sincerely yours,
Blossom Lily Herbert

A TUNE IN MY POCKET

BEAUTY MY SISTER gave me this tape recorder, she said, Fancy my love, which is her best pet name for me, she said, Talk into it, tell it things when you get The Urge. I said, What is The Urge? She said, You know, honey, when you want to talk a lot, but everybody is too busy to listen—that's The Urge.

She said, Do you get what I mean, and I said, Yes, I do, and I love you.

And I love you, she said, and you can talk here and tell this little tape recorder everything. See, she said, you take this and push this button and talk all you want and when you're done, you push this button.

So I said, Okay, I will do it.

And so this is The Urge, and I pushed the button, and I am talking all I want, like Beauty my sister said I could. They are all inside doing things like homework, and Stevie my sister, which is her new name, *Stevie* not Faithful, which she says is a girly name and she is sick of girly names in our family, and she is yelling *again* that we should have a computer, but my mommy said we don't have the money and I told you a million times, so shut up about it, and she says she is too fat and smokes too many cigarettes, and Stevie my sister said, You said it, Mommy, you are a walking bad habit, which was such a funny thing to say, but my mommy didn't laugh, she said, You are just too smart for your own good, Missy, and they were yelling *too much*, so that is why I am outside walking around having The Urge.

To say, uh, uh, I have a lot to say. That is what Mrs. Sokolow my teacher says to me and she is sooo nice. She likes me. She loves me, and I love her. I am a good student for her. And I am the best, fastest-running runner in my class. Ha-ha! That's a halfway joke, because who would be a walking runner? I am not like Randy Parsons, who can never see a joke. *See* a joke is also funny, and I like funny things.

Funny things are my favorite things in the whole world,

19

which is big, and Mallory where I live is small says Mim my sister, but I don't think so. I think Mallory is big with a lot of streets and stores and houses and cars and big buildings like the opera house, which is where people used to get up on the stage and sing, and I think I would like to do that, because I like singing, it is my favorite thing in the whole world, but when I sing, Stevie my sister says, Shut up, you can't carry a tune! And you know what? That makes me *confused*.

Confused is what Mrs. Sokolow my teacher told me, like when I get mad at Stevie my sister because she says a mean thing, but I laugh because *carry a tune* is *sooo* funny. I asked Mrs. Sokolow my teacher can I say, You shut up, too, because I am not carrying a tune in my pocket. She said, Shut up is not nice, Fancy, but maybe you should try that next time and see what happens. So I did. I said to Stevie my sister, You shut up, too, I am not carrying a tune in my pocket, I am not carrying a tune in a bag, I am not carrying a tune in a box. And every time she says, Shut up, you can't carry a tune, I will tell her I am not carrying a tune anywhere!

And I am going to sing right now.

Good-bye!

LIKE VELCRO

IF THE GIRLS are on time, his time, the man sees them as he turns at the corner of Carbon Street onto Fuller Avenue. They will be coming toward him, hopping over snow-clogged sidewalks, all legs and arms and hair, chattering away, seemingly unaware of the rot and filth of Fuller Avenue: the decrepit diner with the smeared windows, the pigeons pecking at the greasy papers clogging the gutter. The man hates pigeons, their noisy, grunting clucks, their strutting walk, the suspicious whir of their wings. Ugly creatures. Disease vectors. Rats with wings. If he had a gun, he'd shoot them all, do a good deed for the world.

He likes the thought. A good deed for the world. He repeats it to himself, watching the girls. *The girls . . . a good deed for the world.* The phrases cling to one another, like Velcro they cling. *The girls . . . a good deed for the world.* As a young boy, he dreamed of doing good deeds— of helping an old lady across a traffic-clogged street or saving a screaming, helpless child from a fiery building. Once he told his mother these dreams of good deeds, and her face flushed, she kissed him and said, "What a very nice person you are!" His parents were older and quiet, and often appeared slightly surprised to see him there in their life.

On his revised route he's obliged only to cross this disgusting street to get to the bus stop, but the girls—poor things!—must walk the full length of the street, all twelve long blocks, to arrive at Mallory Central School. He knows exactly where the school is located. He has walked by the brick building with its ugly, blank-faced annex and rundown trailer, but not too often. It's the kind of place he takes care to avoid. He'd done things so carefully these past couple of years, it would be stupid to be caught hanging around a school. And he's not stupid.

He arrives at the corner of Fuller Avenue and Carbon

Street at precisely the same time every day. If he's lucky, the girls are there to greet him. Although they never even look at him, he likes to think of it that way: they are greeting him with their high voices, and how they toss their hair, and the way in which they bend and hunch against the cold.

He thinks about them as he approaches the corner. Will they be there? His mind tingles, his step lightens. Behind his glasses, fogged by cold, he looks at each one, singles them out, fixes them in his mind. Then, later, at work, he has all of that—all of them—to think about. Musing over the girls makes time pass. Which one does he like the most? He considers, rejects, chooses, changes his opinion, prefers this one, then that one.

Happiness.

MAKING MRS. KALMAN HAPPY

JUST AS YOU'RE leaving school, pretty Mrs. Kalman stops you in the hall and says, "Autumn dear, do you know who I am?"

Of course you know. She's your school counselor. You look at her briefcase and wonder what's in it—must be important stuff. You fidget under her glance and wish you hadn't braided your hair this morning. It's too babyish.

Mrs. Kalman is saying she's been thinking about you.

"Me?" you say.

Mrs. Kalman nods. Is she looking friendly or serious? It's hard to tell, because her face is always the same. "Mr. Spiegleman and I have been talking about you."

That doesn't sound good. You must be in trouble. For the day you were late, maybe. Or maybe Mr. Spiegleman found out you knew more than you told on Oral Report Day, and he's mad.

"Mr. Spiegleman is concerned about you, Autumn. You failed the last two spelling tests."

Why does she have to say that? That's not nice! Those tests were hard and, anyway, what does it matter? You're not a good speller like Mim, who knows everything about all that language arts stuff.

Mrs. Kalman is looking at you like she's waiting for you to say something. What? What are you supposed to say? Your eyes wander up to the white-tiled ceiling. You like ceilings. They are like dreams . . . or stories. Right now, practically over your head, is what some people would call a water stain, but you're seeing a girl's face, her mouth half open, like she's in the middle of talking. Maybe *she's* giving an oral report. You like that idea. The water-stain girl looks like Fancy, who always has her mouth going. Like Stevie would say, Fancy's a walking oral report.

"Autumn!" Mrs. Kalman says in a voice that's a little bit cross. "Hello! Look at me, please."

You drag your eyes down to her. Now you *know* you're

25

in trouble. You're going to get detention. Poppy will laugh about it, except he doesn't laugh very much since he fell off the ladder and walks around all bent over with that neck brace and everything, but Mommy will be plain-out mad. You didn't show Mommy the two failing spelling tests. Your chest is tight. It's like having a stomachache again, only higher.

"Mr. Spiegleman tells me you're just getting by in other subjects," Mrs. Kalman is saying. "He knows you can do better. He says you're not working up to capacity."

"Oh," you say, and you wonder why you're smiling. You don't mean to smile. The smile is just there. You didn't want it. It just popped out on your face.

"Well, what do you think?" Mrs. Kalman says in that sort-of-cross voice.

You shift your backpack. You look at her long blond hair. What are you supposed to say? You failed those tests. You didn't *want* to fail them, but you did. Because you're not special in school like Mim and Beauty. The stomachache in your chest gets worse.

"Capacity," you hear yourself saying. "That's like a spelling word."

"Yes, it is," Mrs. Kalman says. "Can you spell it?"

You concentrate. Ka-pass-a-tee. But you know it begins with a C. You say, *"C-A-P."* Under your breath, you say, "capacity" again, and you try to see the word. You say, *"A-S-A-T-Y."*

"Not quite," Mrs. Kalman says. "You're off by two letters. That's not so bad. Here, I'm going to write it down for you." She takes a little notebook out of her briefcase and writes in it. "Now you can study this word and amaze Mr. Spiegleman when you ace it on a test."

Mrs. Kalman's notebook cover is blue. You say, "Blue is my favorite color." Was that a stupid thing to say?

"Really?" Mrs. Kalman's voice goes all singy, like she's so happy you said that. "Well, guess what, Autumn, this notebook is for you." You stare at her. She says, "It's a present. Don't you like presents?"

You like presents, all right. You like them a lot. You wonder if you should say that. You wonder if you should tell her that your birthday is coming, but because of Poppy's bad back and no job, there won't be money for presents. Mommy told you that already. She warned you, so you wouldn't be disappointed. But she said she would make you a cake, so that part is good.

Mrs. Kalman puts the notebook in your hand. You find

your voice and say, "Thank you."

She pats your head and says, "I want you to use it to write down your thoughts and feelings."

You think, What feelings? What thoughts?

"Make me a promise to write in it every day," Mrs. Kalman says.

Every day? So it isn't a present. It's a school thing, an assignment.

"It's like a blog," Mrs. Kalman says. "You know what a blog is, don't you?" You nod, although you have just a vague idea.

"It's like a blog," she repeats, "only in a notebook, instead of a computer, and just for you, not for the whole world. Private. That's important. Private, personal thoughts and feelings. You do this, and you'll see, you'll like it, and before you know it—" She pauses sort of dramatically, and her voice rises, like Stevie's voice when she gets excited. "Before you know it, you'll be doing better in school!"

"Uh-huh," you say, because you don't know what else to say, and you have to say something.

Mrs. Kalman squeezes your shoulder. "That's my theory, anyway. I hope I'm right, Autumn!" Now she's laughing, and she looks nice when she laughs and tosses her blond hair around like a movie star. "It's up to you to make me happy by proving my theory. All you have to do is write in this notebook every day. Will you do that for me?"

"Okay," you say, and you nod a lot and give her a smile. You like to make people happy, and you hope you can do it for Mrs. Kalman, but what you're thinking is that she *will* look at the notebook, because she's a teacher and that's what teachers do, and then she'll give you a mark, and it will be another bad mark.

HAROLD AND VIOLET

THE ALARM CLOCK brings the man awake. He gets out of bed promptly, stretches, then drops to the floor and does twenty-five push-ups. He's a bit tired at twenty, but he keeps going. He's proud of those push-ups. He was never one of those strong boys with thick shoulders and defined arm muscles, and it wasn't easy working up to twenty-five. So he does his push-ups diligently, only allows himself to take off Sundays.

After the push-ups, he showers, brushes his teeth, and combs his hair, parting it on the left side. Always the left side. Always twenty-five push-ups. Always clean socks, clean underwear, and a change of shirt every three days.

He inspects himself in the mirror, straightens his tie. Always a tie, although it's not a requirement of his job. "A tie shows self-respect." His father's words, one of the few good things his father ever said.

He goes downstairs. The cats are waiting for him. "Good morning!" he says to them. They look at him expectantly. He's hungry, but he feeds them first. "You know," he says, getting the can of cat food from the cupboard, "I think of you guys before myself. You know what that means, don't you?" He looks at them. They look back.

He takes the can opener from the drawer. The cats watch. Sometimes he's lonely, but the cats make it better. He likes the way they watch him, listen to him, and he likes the way he talks to them, like a regular person, like anyone else. The thought passes through his mind that he's a good man. He wishes that someone else knew how he feeds the cats before himself. He would like to hear someone tell him that he's a good man, a good person.

He opens the can of food. The cats follow his every move. They are quiet, concentrated. They aren't shedders or talkers. He had the other kind—noisy, wild, undisciplined. Those cats had to go. They were bad for his health. He would find himself yelling at them, losing control.

"You're different," he tells them. He spoons the food into their bowls. A bowl for each of them. "You're good cats. You listening?" They are.

"Harold. Violet." He calls them to come to their feeding place near the back door

"They say you can't train cats," he tells them, setting the bowls down on the floor, "but I trained you, didn't I?"

He's said it before, but Harold and Violet don't object. They look up at him, then bend to their bowls.

They are named after his parents, whom he hasn't seen or heard from in many years. Harold and Violet, the people, are probably still living in California, San Fernando Valley, same old place, same old house. One of these days he might visit them. He imagines the visit, how he will tell them he has two cats named for them. His father will stare at him, not getting that it's a nice thing the man has done, a good thing, but his mother will be pleased. "You're my boy," she'll say, and she'll stroke his hair, and he'll let her, although he doesn't like to have his head touched.

"You're the best," he tells them. "Chow down. Enjoy yourselves." He pets them briefly.

Now it's his turn. He toasts bread, boils an egg, makes coffee. Harold is grooming himself, licking his paws.

Violet has stretched out in a small patch of sunlight on the floor. "You know how to live," he tells her, although secretly he approves more of Harold, who is so particular about his personal hygiene.

Both these cats are *good*, though, unlike the others. They don't jump up in his lap without an invitation. They don't claw the furniture or yowl at night. He had to go through a great deal of effort, a lot of cats, to get these two excellent ones. A lot of Violets and Harolds, some buried in the previous backyard, some in this backyard.

"How many do you think?" he asks Harold. Violet is sleeping. "Eight? Ten?" He's forgotten the exact number. Fortunately, there are always more cats in the world. And nobody could deny that it's satisfying to bury something and thus enrich the soil. The proof of it is the stand of tall, golden Jerusalem artichokes, which grow so wonderfully over the Violets and Harolds. The flowers are beautiful and, should he so desire, he could dig up the roots and eat them. Nature is a wonderful thing.

CABBAGE HEAD

WHEN BEAUTY ENTERED seventh grade, everything changed for her. She had newly grown breasts, new classmates from all over the city, and all new teachers and classes, but the teacher who captivated her was Mr. Giametti. Paul Giametti, fresh out of college and passionate about teaching these bored Mallory kids. Almost the first thing he said to Beauty's language arts class on the first Friday of the first week was this: "You people, listen up. If I do nothing else this term, I'm going to teach you all to love poetry and dig metaphors."

He was tall and skinny and blond and funny looking, and Beauty fell in love with him at once. Therefore, she fell in love with poetry and metaphors, even before she loved them for themselves. She straightened out of her C-shouldered slump, wowed that Mr. Giametti didn't seem the least bit put off by the groans, the shuffling feet, the loud yawns from the back-of-the-room boys. He stood in front of his desk and, with a little smile, slowly—so they'd get every word—recited, and then wrote on the black-board, the first poem of the semester.

> music
> is a naked lady
> running mad
> through the pure night

No capital letter on the first word. No period at the end. And those words, *naked lady*. Those words, spoken out loud, written for them to stare at, as if they were ordinary, everyday Mallory words. *Naked lady*. The boys hooted and snorted, the girls giggled nervously. A small subset tried to look uplifted and thoughtful, Beauty among them. Almost no one paid attention as Mr. Giametti explained why this sentence was both a poem and a metaphor.

Later Beauty pulled the words back up into her mind.

She replayed them and took them in like a secret invitation to a strange land. The land of poetry, a place not many people wanted to go, certainly not at first. Friday after Friday, Mr. Giametti stubbornly trolled for the class's attention with funny poems and easy poems and more poems with naked lady kind of words. Some parents objected, and by the end of that school year, Mr. Giametti was gone. Beauty mourned his leaving, because all that year, that awful, hideous, painful year, Fridays were what she lived for, waited for, longed for. She was in love with Mr. Giametti, of course, but it was also the shock and surprise and delight of the poems he stubbornly continued to recite to her class. To *her*, she thought, and let herself get lost in the words he brought to them.

Four years later Beauty still remembers some of those poems, especially one called "postcard from cape cod," made up by a woman named Linda Pastan, someone who wrote a lot of poems. Beauty had Googled her on the computer in the library, and she dreamed that someday she'd meet Linda Pastan—not in Mallory, that was for sure—maybe in Chicago, or New York City, which she planned to visit. She imagined her as very kind with long, beautiful gray hair. They would be at some sort of party, and they'd be holding glasses of, yes, wine, and they'd talk.

Beauty: *I love your postcard poem, and I know it by heart.*

Linda Pastan: *Really?*

Beauty: *Yes. I think it's beautiful. It always makes me happy to think about it.*

Linda Pastan: *Would you like to say it for me?*

Beauty: *"just now I saw*
one yellow
butterfly
migrating
across buzzard's bay
how brave I thought
or foolish
like sending
a poem
across months
of silence
and on such
delicate
wings."

That's the good fantasy and the good memory. The bad memory, unfortunately not a fantasy, is the note she found in her locker later that Friday, after Mr. Giametti read them the naked lady poem.

> beauty h
> is an old cabbage
> boiling mad
> on the pure stove

No capital letters. No periods. And funny. Wasn't it funny? She had wanted to be amused by this, wanted to believe that the heat in her face was only suppressed laughter. Wanted to believe the boiling mad part really pleased her. After all, her reputation—as she knew only too well—was not just homely and wrong named, but *prissy*. Wussy. But, look, here was someone who saw her as feisty enough to be *boiling mad*.

"Great!" she heard herself say, and turned over the paper to see a drawing of a girl with a huge head that closely resembled a cabbage. The letters B. H. were encased in a balloon floating nearby and, in the unlikely event that she didn't get it, an arrow from the letters pointed to the drawing.

Kids tramped by. Someone said, "Hi, Beauty." She

answered automatically, fixed a smile on her face. *Cabbage head, that's me.*

The misery of that year had simmered down, but Beauty believed the sting of the memories, the humiliation, would never truly leave her until she left Mallory and changed her life, changed every bit of it, starting with her name. No more Beauty. She would become a Karen or possibly Heather or Kristy.

If she had a regular name like that now, she would be the kind of girl who wore baggy jeans and plain white shirts, who was an average student and sat anonymously in the middle of every classroom, and no one would notice her or her face or her name, ever, for any reason.

In fact, though, she was a better-than-average student and, like most of the girls in Mallory Central School, she wore her shirts colorful and her jeans tight. Her family and other people looked at her as a regular Mallory girl, maybe homelier than most, but ordinary and careful and dependable, not one to make waves or take chances or do anything the least bit unusual. *Oh, really? Well, someday, they'll be surprised. I'll show them!* That was what she'd been thinking for a long time. Was that why last year, secretly and alone, she had taken herself to the tattoo parlor on Locust Street, in a crummy part of town, and why now, on her right thigh, a giant green butterfly (really a moth named Luna) fluttered over a brilliant blue daisy-like flower?

"Not very biologically sound," the tattoo artist had said, holding his needle suspended over her bare thigh. "Sure you want the flower blue?"

"I'm sure," she had said, and closed her eyes, so she wouldn't have to see the needle.

HER HAIR

THE MAN ALWAYS looked at people's hair. You could tell a lot about a person from the hair. Cheyenne, who worked in the next cubicle, had a short, spiky haircut. He hated it, hated her for having it. Girls should look like girls, not boys! One of his birds had long hair, and never wore a hat, no matter how chilly the weather, almost as if she were showing off her hair for him. If she only knew how much that pleased him, her bare head and the length of her hair, and the sheen, and the color, and how thick it was, thick and glossy.

And here she came now, here they all came! His heart quickened, but he didn't alter his pace, or the expression on his face. As he approached from the opposite direction, he studied the one with long hair. The five of them were all there today, all clumped together now on the corner, the gaggle of them, waiting for the light to change, twittering and giggling. The one with long hair was jumping from one foot to the other. Her hair flew out behind her, healthy hair, pretty hair, but too messy.

Yes, too messy for his taste, all that hair just flailing around her head, without even a tie holding it back. Some days it was even worse, looked as if she'd forgotten to comb it. Didn't she know that grooming was important for a lady? If he had a chance, he would certainly tell her that. He would be nice about it, of course, point out how easy it was to stay neat, then offer to give her a trim, even to style her hair. He could do that.

In his mind's eye he saw her sitting meekly in a chair, and himself standing behind her, brushing her hair for her. Brushing from the top to the bottom, his other hand following the brush, smoothing her hair, playing with it a little, lifting strands to sniff, winding it around his hand, winding it tighter and tighter. She would shriek, and he would reassure her, unwind her hair, slowly unwind it.

He thought about this, and then he didn't think it. The

girls crossed the street, and he moved toward his bus stop, banishing the image, pushing it away, although there was nothing wrong with it. Nothing wrong with thoughts. Nothing wrong with his thoughts. They were just thoughts, ripples of the mind. They didn't mean anything.

And there was nothing wrong with looking at the girl, with looking at all of them. If anyone ever asked, he'd say he enjoyed looking at them the way any man would. It was a manly thing to do. He might admit that he was partial to the one with the long hair, because she was more ladylike than the others, and he would be respected for that.

HISSY FITS

HERE IS WHAT you think in your heart, and here is the first thing you write in the notebook Mrs. Kalman gave you. *My name is Autumn Jane Huddle, and this is my privite for me only diary journal. Mommy and Poppy are awful. That's my true privite feeling. Well, Mommy is not so bad, but sometimes I hate her, too. Nobody read this! You are snooping if you read this. Poppy not getting work is making them both like crazy, fighting people. Poppy is sitting out in his truck and Mommy is talking to herself.*

You write that after the fight. You were all at the table, eating supper, when Poppy threw down his fork and swore. "Damn it, I'm fed up with macaroni every day.

44

Can't you make any other damn thing, Blossom?"

You wanted to sink right into the stool or get away or something, but Poppy was looking all around the table, not nice like he always used to be but glaring at everybody, and you didn't dare move. You wouldn't dare say a thing, either, not even *pass the salt please*, with Poppy all mad and everybody looking down at their plates. Even Fancy shut up for a big minute, but not Stevie.

Stevie isn't afraid of *anything*. She got right into the act and made a big hissy fit. "Listen to Daddy," she said, only she didn't *say* it, she screeched it, the way she does. "Me, I'm sick of the same thing, the same old thing, macaroni, macaroni, all the time!"

You always get that I'm-going-to-throw-up, sick-in-the-belly feeling when Stevie has a fit and yells at people, which she does about twenty-three times a day, but you can't help thinking she's kind of brave, too, and you wish you were more like her. Your secret about yourself is that you're a huge scaredy cat. You're scared of so many things, like burglars and lightning and driving across a bridge in a car and going to the dentist, which you didn't do this year, and it's one thing, anyway, to be glad about when your family doesn't have money.

Mommy is sort of like Stevie, yelling a lot, but nicer, except when she gets mad. Then she gets really, really mad and throws things, and sometimes it's funny, like she throws a pot holder or a dish towel, and everybody ducks and tries not to let Mommy see them laughing. But this time, when Poppy said that about the food, she threw a pot right across the room, and it crashed into the wall.

Fancy, who's your favorite sister, sang out. "Lucky, lucky, lucky it didn't hit any person body," and you look at her and sort of smile, because you know nobody will scold her.

Then Beauty said, "Hey, you all, Daddy's back is going to get better, right, Daddy? Like your foot last year, after you fell into that woodchuck hole when you went hunting? And then you can work again, and everything will be okay."

You could see Daddy's face sort of cooling off and getting nice again, and he nodded, and you let out a big breath you didn't even know you'd been holding. After a bit everybody started talking, Mommy even sat down next to you and petted your hair, so you knew she wasn't mad anymore. And everybody ate their supper and was happy.

Except you. Your stomach still hurt, so you asked to be excused, and you went to your room and wrote in your notebook, and then you felt sort of better, but you still didn't want to eat supper.

BEAUTY AND ETHAN: THE MOVIE

BEAUTY WAS ON her way out of school, hurrying to get to her job at the florist shop, when she almost ran into Ethan Boswell, a junior boy she sort of knew from AP World History, who was taking the steps back into school two at a time. He had long legs, and he was on the track team. "Oops, sorry," she said, and stepped aside. So did he. "Double oops," she said, and stepped to the other side. So did he. It was one of those stupid moments that were so stupid they were funny.

Ethan seemed to be holding back a laugh. His nose twitched. Then he dashed around her. That little dance lasted just long enough for Beauty to look closely at

Ethan—he sat way in the back of Mr. Magruder's class and never said much—and to see that he wasn't just another tall and skinny guy who could run, but had a bit of dash. He wore two thin silver rings in one ear and a brilliant rose-colored scarf, like a flag marking him out, tied across his forehead. Not the usual Mallory toughboy or jockboy—or any Malloryboy—getup.

Beauty looked around for her sisters, saw none of them, and kept going, walking fast and wondering why she had never really noticed Ethan Boswell before, when he was so *very* cute. Her heart rose and sank at the same moment. Yes, yes, it was going to be another crush. She'd been holding out against falling again, falling for a boy, falling into the agonizing, thrilling highs and lows of passion. In some corner of her mind, she had held the thought that *not* to have a crush was somehow freeing, but walking west on Midler Avenue, she was talking to Ethan. *Frankly, it was that scarf that captured my heart, that just slayed me!*

But what about her will slay him, knock him over, stop him in his fast run through life? She shifted her backpack, trotted a block, imagined herself running alongside him on the track behind the school. Is that how they'll get started? Maybe. Well, not in real life. Anyway, fast-forward. Fingers linked, she and Ethan are strolling around the duck pond in Lafayette Park. She's asking him about himself. He tells her this and that, but mostly he wants to know about her, because he's that unusual kind of person interested in other people, not just himself.

Maybe she'll ask if he ever wondered about her name. *I bet you did. Bizarre, huh?* Cueing him in that if he had made fun of her name, her face, of *her*, that she understands, really she does. But no, that script is too real. This is a *fantasy*, a movie, and she's actress, director, and scriptwriter, so she can have it anywhichway she pleases. All right then, on with it. Take One, the name scene.

When they named me, my parents were out of their minds, Ethan. An amused tone—she's going for laughs here. *Berserk people! Someone shoulda called the little men in white.* Or maybe a more serious approach? *I have suffered with this name every day of my life.* Whew! Waaay too dramatic. He fingers the silver rings in his ear, nods encouragingly. She notices his ears are large and a little floppy. Sweet. Didn't she read somewhere that big ears are a sign of a sensitive nature? Nonsense, of course, but still. He is *so* sensitive, especially for a boy—but she

50

won't say that; it's sort of sexist.

As she dashed across Oak Street, still unreeling *Beauty and Ethan: The Movie*, Beauty almost did a repeat of the original Ethan scene, the real one, just catching herself short of running straight into someone else.

"Oops, sorry!" she said to the man, who was carrying a grocery bag, and she moved to step out of his way. It was funny, really. A total repeat. She stepped one way, so did he; she stepped in the other direction, so did he. "Double oops!" she said cheerily. At that point a little smile had teased Ethan's mouth, and then there was that cute twitch of his nose, but this man was no Ethan. He looked at her for a moment, almost too long, then his eyes went blank, and he jerked the grocery bag up in his arm and brushed past her.

"Well, and thank you, too," Beauty said to his retreating, gray-coated back. There you have it, folks, a typical, emotionless, middle-aged Mallory type.

Yes, she thought fervently, it would be soul saving to leave this town! Which was exactly why nothing, nothing, *nothing* would change her mind about getting out of Mallory. That was one promise to herself that she would not break, as she had broken other smaller, less important promises—to eat less, to stop obsessing about her name, to drop her crushes on this teacher and that boy. She'd never managed to keep any of those promises for any length of time, but this one was different.

This promise was life or death. Stuck here forever in Mallory, she'd die. It was as simple as that. She'd be alive, but dead. She pulled open the door to the florist shop. The bells chimed. Patrick looked up from arranging a mixed bouquet and greeted her with a smile.

"Patrick," Beauty said. "I ran most of the way. I'm not late, am I?"

PATTERNS

GRADUALLY, AS THE weather warms, as the snow melts, the man's attitude toward the girls alters. Although there are five of them, sometimes only three appear. And then other times, two, with another one lagging far behind. The lack of patterns is upsetting. Is it right that he never knows if they'll be on time, or how many of them he will see on any day, in any week?

He makes a chart. Basic, no frills. He notes the date and how many show up each day. That day it was two of them. The next day all five of them came galloping along. He continues through the week, then the next week and the next. *Two. Five. Three. Three. Four. One. Five. Three.* And so on.

He is looking for a pattern. Surely there's a pattern. He dislikes uncertainty, ambiguity. As the weeks go on, he frets over their lack of system. Over the missing pattern. It perplexes him. Why not make up their minds, do one thing or another, be consistent. He plays with the idea of speaking to them about it, but what would he say? *Girls, I've been watching you.* . . . *Young ladies, why do you keep shifting the numbers on me.* . . . *Listen, girls, you're upsetting me with your constantly changing numbers.* . . . He mulls over the possibilities, but eventually discards them all. He's no fool.

THE ONE PERSON IN THE WORLD

SATURDAY MORNING, before you're even out of bed, Fancy finds the notebook with the blue cover that Mrs. Kalman gave you. Last night, after you wrote in it, you forgot to hide the notebook, and now Fancy's got it, and she's opening it. She's in her nightgown and her feet are bare, and she's got a bad case of bed hair, which you usually think is so cute on her, but not now.

"Don't you read that," you warn, kicking off your blankets. "That's mine. Give it back to me right now."

Fancy backs away, acting like she didn't hear you or doesn't understand or something. "Did you get this cute notebook for me?" she chirps, all innocent. "I love it." She

55

kisses the notebook, and then she grabs you and lays one of her big, squishy wet kisses on your cheek. "Thank you, thank you, thank you, Autumn my sister. It's *sooo* cute. I can draw pictures in this notebook. I'll draw you a picture."

You jump out of bed and say in a really stern voice, "Give me my notebook, Fancy."

"Mine," she says, and she quick swishes it behind her back with that sly look on her face that you just hate, hate, *hate*. Like she's putting something over on you, like she's smarter than you, which she isn't, and you know it and she knows it. You reach around her for the notebook, but she dodges, giggling. "Hee hee hee hee!"

"Give it to me, Fancy, give it back to me right now," you order.

"Will you two shut up!" Stevie is thrashing around on the top bunk. "I'm trying to sleep here. Autumn, let her have the crummy notebook."

Okay, now you're getting mad, and you want to yell back at Stevie, but you don't, because what if she has one of her awful fits and everything gets messed up, and Mommy *orders* you to give Fancy the notebook, which you will have to do, because Fancy is special needs. Ugh!

"Fancy," you say, and you try to make your voice soft and nice like Mim's. "Mrs. Kalman gave that notebook to me. *Personal*, to me. Which means she didn't want anyone else to have it." You take a big breath and say, "Okay, Fancy? Does that make sense to you?" Which is what Mim says when she explains something to make people stop fighting. You're being very grown-up and mature about this, and you think Fancy should respect that.

Instead, her lower lip droops, and she gets all sad and says, "You don't want me to have this cute notebook. You're being mean to me. I'm going to tell Mommy you're being sooo mean to me."

Mean? That is just *too much*. You're always nice to Fancy, you take care of her all the time, you take her to Lafayette Park, you let her dawdle around looking at the ducks, you tell her stories at night. And now she's saying you're mean?

"I am not being mean!" You can't help it, you just have to shout. "Give me the notebook! Give it to me now, you stinking brat."

"Uh-oh, bad word, bad word," Fancy cries, her mouth all spitty. "I'm going to tell Mommy, I'm going to tell."

On the top bunk Stevie flops around. "Euuu, I hate you

both. Shut up! Shut up, you two brats!"

Fancy makes a scared face and sinks to the floor, and you sink down next to her and cross your legs underneath your nightgown. "Shh," Fancy says. "Stevie wants to sleep."

"I know that," you whisper back. "And I know Mrs. Kalman will be mad if I give you the notebook. She said it's for me to write my private thoughts. She made me *promise* to do that."

"Promise? Oooh. O!" Fancy sighs deeply. "Mrs. Sokolow my teacher says promises are, are—"

You say, "Important?" She shakes her head. "Precious?" She shakes her head. You think, and then you say, "Sacred?" which was a spelling word last week, which you didn't get right, you put in an extra *c*, but you know what it means, and guess what, that's the word Fancy is thinking of.

"Yes! Sacred. That's what Mrs. Sokolow my teacher says. Promises are sacred, which means you have to keep them. You must, you must, you must."

"Yes," you say, "Mrs. Sokolow is right," and you lean closer and you say in your most serious voice, "If you keep that notebook, Fancy, it will be *your fault* that I break my sacred promise."

Slowly, slowly, she brings the notebook out from behind her back. "Good girl," you say, and you reach for it, but she snatches it back and puts it behind her again.

"Fancy!" you say in a mean voice. "Give it!"

"If I give it to you," she says, "you have to tell me a story tonight." You nod okay. "You have to promise sacred," she says, "and no saying you're too sleepy for stories." You nod okay again. You're breathing hard. She's driving you *crazy*!

"I will make you keep your promise," she says, and she still doesn't give you the notebook. She's got that look on her face again, her mouth pursed up tight as if she's biting a smile, and her eyes jumping all around. You hate that look.

"I'm your big sister," she says, "I am bigger than you, I am one and one-half years older than you, and if you don't keep your promise, I will beat your butt."

You would like to beat *her* butt. You reach around her, shoving her and wrestling for the notebook, and she yells, "Okay, take it, mean sister. See if I care, you mean, mean, mean sister!"

You leap to your feet. "I am not mean," you yell. You've got the notebook, but your feelings are so hurt, you're ready to cry. "I am not mean!"

"Autumn!" Stevie leans over the side of the bunk bed. "For the last time, shut *up*." She reaches out and pulls your hair hard, like she wants to pull it right off your head, and you can't stand it, and you scream, "I hate you, Stevie," and sink down on the floor, crying.

And then Mim is there, in her pj's. You didn't hear her come down the stairs, you didn't hear her in the hall, you didn't hear her pad into the room, she's just here, standing on her toes to pat Stevie's head and whispering to her, like *Stevie* is the one who needs comforting.

"Mim," you sob, "Stevie pulled my hair, and it's not my fault, and Fancy took my notebook, and—"

"I just borrowed it for one minute." Fancy doesn't even let you finish. "And I gave it back. I gave it back, Mim, I was good. I'm *good*," Fancy says, "I'm a good girl!" She tilts her head and smiles like she's looking at herself in a mirror and loving herself.

"Come here, you two," Mim says, "let's have a talk."

"Oh, yes, I love a talk," Fancy says, and she sits right down on the floor near the window next to Mim, who crooks a finger at you.

After a moment you crawl over and sit down on the other side of Mim, and you say, "What do you want to talk about?" You know you sound sulky, but you can't help it. Why isn't anybody on your side?

"You can each tell me what happened," Mim says in her soft voice that you practically have to lean forward to hear, "but only one at a time can speak. The other one has to wait for her turn, okay?" She looks at you, and her look isn't anything like her voice; it's a hard look.

So you say, "Okay," even though you know it's *impossible* to keep still when Fancy's mouth starts going. It is so wicked hard you almost can't do it, you almost have to say *something*. It's like wanting to pee, it has to come out, doesn't it? And when Fancy says you *gave* her the notebook, you almost burst, but Mim gives you another one of those looks you hate, with her lips all pressed tight.

Finally it's your turn to talk, and you tell Mim how Fancy *took* your notebook, without permission, and how it's private and all that, and now Fancy has to keep quiet and just listen to you, and she keeps wriggling around and raising her hand, but Mim just shakes her head and pats Fancy's hand. And you talk and talk and tell *everything*. When you're done, Mim says, "Hmm" and "I see," and she doesn't make Fancy apologize or anything. Instead, she says for you and Fancy to each think of something nice to say about the other.

"I can't think of anything," you say, which isn't really true, but you are still a little bit mad at Fancy. Then you sigh and say, "Uh, well, okay. Lots of times she makes me laugh and be cheerful."

"Yeah," Mim says. "So true! Your turn now, Fancy."

"I have two funny parts," she says. "Part One! Autumn tells me the best stories of anybody in the world. Part Two! A funny story came in my head that *you*"—she giggles and flattens her hand against Mim's nose—"make your boyfriend be quiet all the time and listen to you talk, talk, talk."

"That is funny, except I don't have a boyfriend," Mim says.

"Yes, you do," Fancy says. "All girls have boyfriends."

"No, they don't," Mim says. And she laughs.

"Yes, yes, yes, they do," Fancy says. "And you have to have a boyfriend, Mim my sister, because you are sooo pretty, and boys like pretty ladies and girls, and someday I will be a pretty lady and have a boyfriend, and he will kiss me like this." She makes a fat fish mouth and loud, smacky kissing sounds.

"Fancy, don't be thinking about boys all the time," you say. "You have to think about school and learning stuff."

Mim gives you that nice look that means, *Good for you, Autumn, we all have to watch out for Fancy.* Then she says in her soft voice, "I know you want some alone time to write in your notebook, Autumn," and she tells Fancy to come down to the kitchen with her and she will make hot chocolate. Fancy bounces to her feet and takes Mim's hand, and they both leave the room.

You can't believe it! Mim didn't even ask if you want hot chocolate, too. Which you do! When you think how much you love hot chocolate and how hot chocolate would be *so perfect* right now, tears well up in your eyes, and you fling yourself on your bed. You pull the pillow over your face, and you mumble, "I'm sorry. I'm sorry. I'm sorry."

What are you sorry for? *Everything.* You're sorry you called Fancy a stinking brat, you're sorry that you told Stevie you hated her, and you're sorry that what you write in the notebook is so stupid, but most of all you're sorry for yourself, because *they*—your parents, your sisters—don't love you. At least not very much, at least not enough, and not the way you want them to love you—as if you're the one person in the world who really matters.

BIG MAD BEE

HELLO, HELLO, HELLO, I'm having The Urge because I'm mad. I am *sooo* mad. I am mad like a big mad bee, because my mommy makes me stay home and on our street all the time, like right now, I can just stay on our sidewalk, because everyone is busy and it's Saturday and no school. She says later *maybe* I can go for candy at Mrs. Wilkins's nice little store on the corner, and *maybe* I can go to Lafayette Park with Autumn my sister, but she says probably not the park because she worries I'll get my feet wet and get sick, like last winter when I got pneumonia and she had to take me to the doctor and give me medicine.

My mommy worries about everything in the whole world. She worries too much! That's what I say. Every day in the world, she says, Fancy don't just run across the street and don't talk to strangers and don't go in the woods at the park and get your feet wet and don't eat too much candy and don't go out without your boots on and did you remember to brush your teeth and did you do your work in school today. She has a million kazillion worries about me and she says I give her gray hair but she puts stuff on her hair from the drugstore and it isn't gray it's black and sometimes it's red and I laugh when she says gray hair.

But I forgot to tell her that this cute person Michael came to my class and told about the Special Olympics in Syracuse, which we could go to on the bus because Mrs. Sokolow my teacher said we should think about it, Fancy, you're such a good runner I bet you could win a medal, and here's the funny thing, a medal is metal, but it sounds like when people call me mental—

Whoa, girl! Whoa, girl! I say that to myself when I get mixed up, and then I have to go back to Go, like in Monopoly, which is my favorite game in the whole world because I can be a rich person in Monopoly and have houses and five hundred dollars, but it's not real money because if it was real money I would give it to Mommy and Poppy and make them happy. I love Mommy and Poppy, and I love my sisters, and I love jokes and funny things. I have a big sense of fun and Mrs. Sokolow my teacher says, Good for you, Fancy, you enjoy life, and she gives me a hug when I make a joke. And that's all I have Urge right now. Thank you. Good-bye. I love you, I will kiss you. Ha-ha! Kissing a tape recorder! I am *sooo* funny and I make myself laugh. I love me. I love everybody.

MY BOY

SINCE THAT AFTERNOON when she almost ran into Ethan Boswell, Beauty had been watching him. *Beauty and Ethan: The Movie, Part Two*. Beauty Herbert, PI, keen observer of Ethan Boswell. Naturally, it was a covert business, a secret operation. Naturally, it was juvenile, but what was to be done about that? All this stuff had always gone on in her head, and it still did. Replacement for real life.

Was Ethan shy? He fooled around like the other boys, bumping, crashing, making his presence known, but he also stuttered, and he blushed. He was not the sort of boy on whom, through the years, Beauty had secretly crushed and always privately dubbed *My Boy*. Ethan didn't fit the mold. It was a different kind of crush. Hearing Ethan in class stumbling on a word turned Beauty's heart tender toward him. So this is what happened, this is how it went: she watched him, she listened to him, she yearned for him, and then she wanted him. But so what? Her fate was to be forever unkissed, forever untouched, forever unable to do anything about it.

That's what she thought until that day in March when she went for a walk—for once, no work, no sisters, no one needing her, and the woods at the edge of town beckoning.

THE RAILROAD BRIDGE

THE MAN WALKS down this scruffy side street often on the weekends. He walks past the faded hardware store, past the video store specializing in "adult movies," past the tattoo parlor, its green neon sign blinking day and night, and then comes to the Eminent Diner with its red dome and greasy windows.

He enters the diner. He likes the food here; it's plain and solid, like his mother's food. As always, it's crowded and noisy and he knows no one, and no one knows him. Which is just the way he wants it, and why he puts up with the noise and the crowds.

He finds an empty booth. A boy wearing jeans and a

T-shirt that says DO I LOOK LIKE I CARE? fills the water glass. The waitress appears. "Hi, hon. What can I get you?"

"Beef stew, please. And an order of mashed potatoes."

"Anything else?"

"Coffee."

"Right away, hon."

When his order comes, he cuts the meat into small chunks and pushes aside the carrots, the same gestures he always made with his mother's beef stew.

When he leaves the diner, he walks a few more blocks to the old railroad bridge over the river. He stands at the entrance to the bridge, gathering his courage. His fear of heights is a deep shame to him. The narrow pedestrian catwalk is little more than two boards loosely laid side by side, and through the gap between the boards, which creak warningly as he steps onto them, he tries not to look at the fast-flowing river below.

He walks steadily, carefully, one foot before the other. Is that a train whistle he hears? He falters; one foot slips off the walkway. His chest tightens. He imagines himself running as the train bears down on him, the engineer futilely blowing the whistle, himself running, stumbling, and falling, falling through the wide-open bridge supports into the raging water.

His heart is whacking away in his chest. Then he says, "Trains don't come at this time." He says it out loud, he says it firmly, as befits a rational man. He repeats it. "Trains don't come at this time." He looks quickly around to make sure no one is there to hear him talking to himself. His father's father died of a heart attack, so did two uncles, all of them in their mid-forties. His age. He draws in a deep, faltering breath, then another and another. Finally he continues to walk across the bridge, and he makes it to the other side, untouched. Safe. He makes it, as he has made it every other time he's walked here, but never without imagining falling to his death on the rocks in the river below.

That walk puts period to the weekend.

Monday morning he's at the usual corner at the usual time. He doesn't see any of the girls. The next morning he sees all five of them. He should be elated, yet it's come about that now he doesn't care for so many of them at once. Five! Too many, too many!

They rush past him, chattering, their backpacks bouncing. They don't notice him. He could be a light pole they're passing. The one who talks too much almost knocked into him one day. She didn't apologize, just shouted something at the others and raced on. He doesn't like her. He doesn't like the awkward way she runs, her feet turning in. There's something stupid in her face. He wouldn't choose her. That's definite.

He doesn't like the big one, either, the tall homely one that he's seen other places. He really doesn't care for her at all. It isn't the homeliness, per se. He isn't prejudiced that way. After all, he knows he's no prize in the face department, although the mustache he's grown these past months has definitely done something for him. The big girl, though, is too big, too tall. She has breasts. He doesn't like breasts. He especially doesn't like those big puffy ones, the ones that stick out like balloons.

He eliminates her, and he eliminates the stupid one. He just won't think about them. That's a relief. It clears matters up. He can concentrate on the other three, which makes everything neater, more orderly. Only three. Funny that he was so delighted at first with five. But everything changes, doesn't it? That's the way life is. Nothing stays the same. You can try and try to keep things in order—and he does—but something is inevitably always going to screw it up. Throw a monkey wrench in the works. You have to be clever to stay on your feet, to keep out of the eye of the storm, and he is clever. He's got everything under control.

He strides, swinging his arms. An aerobic walk and the delicious murmuring of his mind. The delicious questions. Which one does he like the best? Which one is his favorite? For a while it's been the small, quiet one, but there isn't much of her. She's a skinny thing, the only skinny one among them. Doesn't appeal.

So it comes down to the youngest one—he thinks she's the youngest—with the long brown hair or the sulky-looking one with the fat lips and cute little belly sticking out of her jeans. He goes back and forth in his mind. This one. That one. Hair girl. Belly girl. Which one? It's only a game. It doesn't mean anything. He's only looking, letting his thoughts play, playing with his thoughts. Nothing wrong with that. It gives an interesting flavor to his days, makes him step out of the house each morning with something to look forward to. And during the day, he can think about them, pass the two of them through his mind. All in his mind. Touch her hair. Touch her belly. Which one? Belly Girl or Hair Girl. All in his mind. And it makes the time pass.

THANK YOU FOR THE NIGHTMARE

"AUTUMN . . . AUTUMN . . ." Someone's calling you. You try to answer, but your mouth is glued shut, and it's so stupid not being able to talk that you burst out of your dream. "Whew!" you say into the darkness, joyful at your quick getaway. Then you realize that someone *is* calling your name. It's Stevie, leaning over from the top bunk.

"What's the matter?" you ask, but you know: Stevie had a nightmare. Every time Stevie has a nightmare, she wakes you up. Not Fancy or Mim or Beauty. Only you. "Want me to come up?" you say, which is what you always say, and you're already pushing aside the covers and

74

climbing up into her bed. "Was it a really bad nightmare?" you ask, snuggling in next to her and yanking a little at the covers, which she's hogging as usual.

"It wasn't a *good* nightmare," she says, and bumps her butt into you for asking such a dumb question. "It was horrible," she says, "it was raining like crazy, and it was dark, and I saw Poppy on the roof. I could see *everything*, it was so real. Poppy was wearing those striped overalls with the big pockets? And he was just set to go down the ladder, and then he slipped, his foot slipped right off the ladder."

Your stomach is going all yucky, like you want to throw up, like you're standing there in the rain, too, watching Poppy on the ladder, like it's not even a dream. You cuddle in closer to Stevie, and you must have fallen asleep for a moment, because the next thing you know, she's saying, ". . . wanted to save him, but I couldn't, I just had to stand there and watch him fall and smash into the ground. He looked *dead*, he just lay there, he didn't move."

Stevie's voice goes high, like she's going to cry, except she never cries. "It was so *real*. It was raining that afternoon when Poppy fell, remember? I could hear the rain hitting the metal roof. I even saw the color of the roof. Green."

You remember that it was still raining two days later, when you all went to look at that green metal roof, Poppy with his neck in a brace and his arm in a sling. Stevie is starting to tell the whole dream again, but quick, before she can get to the dead part, which will make you cry, you know it will, you say, "Stevie! Poppy is okay! He's getting better. He's right down the hall with Mommy, in their bed. It was just a dream, Stevie."

"I know that, Autumn," she snaps. "I'm just trying to tell you something, I'm trying to tell you how horrible it was."

Now she sounds like herself, ready to bite your head off, and for once you're glad of it. Your arm is around her waist, and your nose is in her hair, and you say, "Your hair smells really good. Is it a new shampoo?"

For a moment Stevie doesn't answer, and you think she's going to get mad that you changed the subject, but then she says, "Same cheap old stuff that cheap old Mommy always buys. You know the way she squeezes every last drop out of the detergent? The bottle is empty, you know it's empty, everyone knows it's empty, but *she* turns it upside down and squeezes and squeezes, just in case there's one little drop left."

"She does the same thing with the milk," you say.

"And the juice," Stevie says.

"And the salad oil," you say.

"And if you catch her at it," Stevie says, "she'll tell you that Grandma told her the most important thing she ever learned."

And then, at exactly the same moment, like a perfect chorus, the two of you say it together, just the way Mommy says it, in her hoarse voice: "Waste not, want not!"

It's bad to make fun of Mommy, you know you shouldn't do it, but you squeal with laughter, and just then, when you're all full of love for Stevie, and all perky and proud that you were so clever in helping her forget her nightmare, just then she says, "Go back to your own bed, you're sweaty and stinky."

"I was going to sleep with you," you say, and you try to snuggle in closer.

She gives you a little shove. "I can't sleep with you puffing in my ear like that."

"You didn't even thank me for the nightmare—"

"Thank you for the nightmare!" Stevie's laughing again, but at you, this time. "Thank you, thank you, okay? *Go.*"

So you climb back down to your own bed, which is cold now, and you try to get comfortable, but you're so awake you can't sleep. Then you hear Stevie snoring away above you, and it's not fair! You get all teary thinking how Stevie kicked you out of her bed after you were so nice to her, and you decide you'll never help her with another nightmare, never, *ever*. And that's the last thing you remember until morning comes.

SOMETHING DRASTIC
THIS WAY COMES

THAT DAY WHEN Beauty entered the woods was one of those rare early April days when the temperature suddenly shoots up twenty degrees, and winter briefly turns into spring. Beauty was stealing a couple of hours for herself, a chunk of time free of her job at the florist shop, free of her sisters and her mother's endless needs. The sun had been in and out all day, and the ice on Newton's Pond, where Beauty and her sisters skated every winter, was soft. In the coldest months Beauty could walk across the long frozen pond without a thought, but now she went around it and past the boulder that looked like a hunched-over giant. As a child, she had thought nothing in the world could be bigger than that boulder. She patted it and turned into the woods and onto the worn path that led to the top of Farley Mountain.

Mountain? Not really. Just a hill, although a pretty big hill. A half hour's climb, and you had a 360-degree view of the countryside. Bears lived here, and stories about them were rampant. A bear coming down into Mallory and knocking on someone's plate-glass door, bears in pairs rampaging through garbage, bears chasing hikers and sometimes catching them. You could believe the stories or not, but last year, in late summer, a bear had happened upon Beauty—or she had happened upon the bear—when she'd been on this same trail. Maybe she'd cried out. She'd never been exactly sure of what happened, except that she'd barely had time to be scared when the bear turned around and lumbered off.

"Huh," her father had said when she came home and told the story, "old Mr. Bear was more scared of you than you was of him." And he'd reassured her that black bears, the kind that inhabited their woods and hills, were not aggressive. "Pretty harmless," he said. "Leave 'em alone, and they'll leave you alone. They sure don't want to eat you. They favor berries and things like that. Only thing is, you don't want to meet up with a mama, that might be another story."

Beauty had all this in mind as she moved up the sodden path. The trees were still bare, the bark just beginning to show a reddish tint. All at once the wind came up, and glancing at the sky, she saw thick wads of gray clouds scudding from north to west. The weather was going to change. She wrapped her scarf more securely around her neck and kept moving.

At the top the sun was shining again, but it was colder up here, windier, too. She stood on a rock and looked out at the immense and distant world. This moment was what she had come for: the radiant sense of being somewhere else, far above and out of and beyond her everyday life, the life that, at one and the same time, held her up and pulled her down. She stood there, buffeted by the wind, her arms wrapped around herself, lost in a dream of the future. Finally she looked at her watch and started back.

At the base of the hill, she slowed and walked quietly as she approached a small clearing where, at various times, she had seen deer, grouse, and wild turkey. If she saw deer, her father would want to hear about it. It would start him thinking about next fall, when he'd go hunting. His back should be better by then, and—

The thought was abruptly cut off. People were in the clearing. Two people, a man and a woman, wrapped together, locked in a kiss, the man's hands around the woman's bare waist, her hands around his face.

Wait. Not a man and a woman. A boy and a girl. No, not that, either. A boy and her sister. Her little sister Stevie.

The hands gripping the boy's face, as if holding him to her by sheer force, were Stevie's hands. And the hands that were creeping down the back of Stevie's jeans were the boy's hands.

At once, without thinking, Beauty reversed herself and went running back up the path, not quiet now, nothing in her mind but running from the sight of her little sister passionately kissing the boy, hugging his head, the sight of the boy's hand down the back of her little sister's pants.

That night she lay in bed, wakeful, one arm over her eyes. What a fool she was, believing that she needed no one, that all the painful moments she dragged herself through, and had still to drag herself through, meant nothing. Believing that it was good to hold out to have a real life until she escaped Mallory. *Fool. Fool!*

Everything had changed in that moment of seeing her

sister wrapped around the boy.

Stevie—passionate, demanding, infuriating Stevie—who was barely out of childhood, already had what Beauty, on her way to adulthood, had never had, which was—well, what? A relationship? Love? Sex? All of the above? Yes. *Yes, yes, yes.*

The name and face of Ethan Boswell came into her mind. Something has to change, she thought. *Something drastic this way comes.* The words hummed in her ears. From a poem, wasn't it, something that Mr. Giametti had read to them . . . Mr. Giametti, dear Mr. G who had landed in Mallory like a rocket . . . She saw that rocket hurtling through space . . . rocket with tail of fire . . . rocket running . . . Odd, she thought, then *she* was running, leaping into the air, and she was naked, but that was all right, because she was running over the bridge out of Mallory, and now she was in a classroom, and it all made sense, it was all wonderful, she was joyous, laughing, and then someone was kissing her, holding her face tenderly, kissing her, kissing her. . . .

In the morning she remembered the dream, the kiss. Oh, God. Oh, God. That kiss. It was so sweet. So sweet.

WALK LIKE A ROBOT

THE MAN STRAIGHTENS his tie, wipes his lips one more time, and checks to make sure the gas jets are turned off. He locks the door behind him and walks briskly past the empty lot that takes up most of the street. A beautiful day, the blue sky, the trees sparkling from last night's rain. The air is fresh this morning. He thinks about the girls. His heart quickens in anticipation, but he walks steadily, neither hastening nor slowing his steps. Long ago, someone cruel—one of the many cruel people he's known in his life—yes, including his father—told him he walked like a robot. The remark hurt his feelings deeply. He couldn't forget it. He had wiped the name of that boy

84

from his memory, but he remembered the voice, the sneer on the face.

He pushes away the memory. He prides himself on being rational, not wasting his time on useless memories, on sentiment. He lives an orderly life, a well-regulated life, and now a habitual part of that life is thinking about the girls. *Thinking.* That's all he's doing. No one can accuse him for thinking.

He hopes to see his two favorites today. The pretty one with the belly has been in the lead for a while, even though her teeth stick out, but last week he heard her yelling at the others. She lost out with him that day. Still and all he likes her and keeps her in his mind, along with the little one with the long hair and the brimming eyes. It's between those two now. Which one is his favorite? The tantalizing question. Maybe today he'll make up his mind.

MISS PRISS

AS THEY LEFT the house Monday morning, Beauty touched Stevie on the back and said, "Walk with me." Early she had awakened to the reproachful thought that she was neglectful, so focused on her own dreary little wants and fantasies that she had overlooked the danger her little sister was headed for. She meant to make up for that right now. "I want to talk to you," she said.

"And I want to talk to you." Stevie stomped down the porch steps. "I have a bone to pick with you," she said as they walked two and three abreast toward Elm Street.

"Me? A bone to pick with me? About what?" What notion had gotten into Stevie's mind now? The girl always had some grievance or other hanging about.

"Me to know, you to find out." Stevie's slightly slanted eyes glittered. She flung her scarf tighter around her neck. "You'll hear. Don't be in such a hurry."

The five of them walked to the corner in a clump, Fancy chattering as usual. It was not quite raining, but the air was wet and heavy, and the trees glistened. The snow was rapidly disappearing, although the icy mounds along the roads remained as dirty as ever from car exhaust.

"So who goes first?" Beauty said.

"Me," Stevie answered like a shot. "Me!"

"Go ahead, I'm listening," Beauty said. At the same time she was counting heads: Fancy was right behind her, Autumn and Mim walking ahead. She heard them working on Autumn's spelling. "Sarcophagus," Mim said, and Beauty winced as Autumn confidently rattled off, "*S-A-R-C-U-F-G-U-S!*"

"I saw you," Stevie said. "I saw you!"

"What do you mean, saw me? Where? What are you talking about?" But she knew, and her heart set up a frightful clatter.

"I saw you spying on me." Stevie's eyes darkened.

"Spying? Are you crazy?"

"Don't act so innocent. In the park. I saw you. Peeping at me!"

"Stevie. I was not spying. I was out for a walk, I was coming down from the top of Farley's, and there you were. I went away. I didn't hang around! The moment I saw you, I left. Did you see me? Did you see me run away?"

"Yes, I saw you. That's why you ran, because I spotted you. How long were you there, spying on me?"

"Stop it," Beauty said. "Just stop that. I wasn't spying. I saw you and . . . and . . . what I want to know is, what's going on with you? We should have a talk about"—she faltered just for a moment—"about sex."

"Oh, no way!" Stevie grabbed the straps of her backpack and pulled at them. "I don't need any talks about that."

"He had his hands all over you," Beauty said. Her ribs ached. Or maybe it was her heart. Did she sound like a horrible, jealous person? "His hands were down your pants."

"What'd you do, stand there and take notes?" Stevie said, smiling scornfully.

Beauty drew in a deep breath and told herself to stop, but could not keep from saying, "What are you doing with

88

him? I'm worried about you. Are you two—"

"Are we *doing it*? Gasp," Stevie mocked. "It's none of your business, but I'll tell you, anyway. No, dear sister, Miss Priss, who can't say *screwing*, I am not doing it."

Was she lying? Stevie often lied. "All right," Beauty said. "I'm glad to hear that, because you're too young to get going like that. I don't want you to get into . . . into . . . dangerous waters."

"How would you even know what's dangerous?" Stevie said, her eyes gleaming. "You've never even had a boyfriend. And in case you forgot, you're not my mother."

"Oh, stop," Beauty said again, futilely, and she turned around to check on Fancy. "Fancy," Beauty called. She had stopped to talk to a little black dog. "Come on. You're going to be late."

"What if she is?" Stevie said. "You spoil her. She's got to learn to take care of herself."

Beauty went to Fancy and took her hand. "Come on, honey, there's not enough time to dawdle."

They walked quickly toward the others, who were waiting for them at the corner.

"I love that dog," Fancy said. "I kissed her and she kissed me back."

"You shouldn't be kissing strange dogs."

"I know that," Fancy said. "Good for me for knowing that. Mrs. Sokolow my teacher will be proud of me."

Traffic was heavy on the corner of Dix Avenue. A cluster of people was waiting at the bus stop across the street. "If it wasn't for you, we would have been across already," Stevie said to Fancy. "I better not be late for play rehearsal."

Beauty wanted to shush her but decided not to. She didn't need another fight with Stevie. A man in a gray overcoat and a gray fedora, very old-fashioned looking, stood just behind them, also waiting to cross. Beauty glanced at him for a moment, then turned away. There was a lull in the traffic, and she said, "Okay, let's go," and they all crossed, Stevie's stiff little shoulders in her bright blue jacket leading the way.

FACE LIKE A POTATO

WHAT LUCK, the man thinks. Here he is, standing on the corner, behind his five birds and so close he can smell them. The one the man likes least, the big one with the face like a potato, smells of cheap perfume. She herds the others along like a sheepdog. She is a dog. He doesn't wish to waste his time on her, doesn't want to even think about her, but there's a certain fascination in her homeliness. He stares at the back of her head. Underneath that long braid of hair, even her neck is ugly. Her Ugliness. He likes the way that sounds. It accounts for her, puts the name and the face and the body all together nicely. *Her Ugliness*.

Now he thinks about naming the others. The one who lags behind and talks without stopping and this morning smelled of breakfast eggs—that's easy. Her Dumbness. Or . . . wait, would Her Dimness be a better name? *Her Dumbness. Her Dimness.* Which one?

When he clocks in at work, the two names are still reverberating.

"Hey ho!" It's Violet, the computer whiz girl. Not really a girl, she has streaky gray hair, a too big and too white smile that chills him. She taps him on the shoulder. "Hey ho," she says again. "What's on your mind this morning? How are you? Have a good weekend?"

A shudder goes through him. He half bows, twitches his cheeks into a smile. "I'm good. How about you?" He knows how to say nothing while making the right sounds. It's a game that he's forced to play to keep them all satisfied. *How are you? I'm good. And you? Good. Isn't it a great day? We deserve some sun. You're so right. Spring is on the way. And about time. Well, have a good one.* All the inane, meaningless noises people make that pass for intelligent conversation. They might as well be pigs grunting in the pen.

In his office he sits down at his desk. Violet walks by his

cubicle and gives him another big white smile. It strikes him that *Violet* is Her Dumbness. Of course. Which means the talky one is *Her Dimness*. Perfect. He turns on his computer, satisfied.

THE ORDEAL

OPENING HER LOCKER after lunch, Beauty dawdled, watching Ethan at his locker taking out books, stuffing them in his backpack. Slowly she zipped her backpack and glanced at him again. Beauty Huddle, Secret Agent of Love. Then came an image of herself leaping on Ethan, grabbing his head, mashing their mouths together. Her mind was *ridiculous*. She could barely bring herself to say hi when she saw him in the halls, not very likely that she'd be leaping on him.

But what about that *drastic action*? Was now the time? If not now, when? She was always putting it off. Her belly lurched, and then she hurled herself—or so it seemed to her—across the space between them. "Uh, hey, Ethan," she said. And it came out timidly, softly, as if she didn't mean it. He didn't turn, did nothing to show that he had even heard her. "Ethan," she said in a desperately cheerful voice. "How's it going?"

"Uh, what?" He banged his locker shut, and he turned to look at her.

"How's it going?" she said again, with a terrified smile.

"Oh. Good," he said. "Yeah, good."

Gathering herself, she said, "What about that history test? Mean, wasn't it?"

"Whew!" He blew air out through his mouth. "Magruder knows how to k-k-k-*kill* us."

"I know. It's true, so true."

"I don't know how I did. Maybe I did okay." His eyes were light blue. "I like that h-h-h-history stuff."

"Yeah," she said, "me, too." And then running the sentences together, as if they were one thought, "He's a good teacher I'm Beauty Herbert."

He nodded. "I know."

Did he mean he knew Mr. Magruder was a good teacher? Or did he mean he knew her name? That was it—he knew her name. Of course he did. Everyone knew

95

everyone in this school. Still, wasn't it amazing? He knew her name! All this raced through her mind and what came out of her mouth, as if it were a brilliant new truth, was: "And you're Ethan Boswell."

"I am."

"I sound like an idiot," she said. "I'm scared. Sorry. Sorry! I want to ask you something."

"Scared? Scared of me?"

"Uh-huh. Worse, now that I've confessed."

"I guess I can be pretty s-s-s-scary."

"No, no, it's not—I didn't mean—I—uh—" At this last groaning sound that she made, she shook her head in despair and closed her eyes and prayed and said, "Can we just pretend I never said anything? Go away, Ethan. Don't look at me. Forget I ever opened my mouth and said such stupid, idiotic things. Good-bye. Are you gone?"

She pressed her lips together and opened her eyes. He was still there. He was watching her. He hadn't run away. He was waiting.

Hot. It was suddenly so hot. She wanted to tear off her sweater, tear off all her clothes. They were looking at each other, and she had the impression that they were speaking without words, that they were telling each other something important. People pushed by. Shouts. Lockers slam-ming. It was all far away.

"So . . . what was it?" he asked.

"What was what?" She was dazed by the look they had just shared.

"What you wanted t-t-t-*to* ask me."

"What I wanted to ask you?" She sucked in air. "Oh. Okay. Can I buy you a coffee? After school. I mean I'll drink some, too. I mean, I won't drink yours. Oh, Lord. I should just shoot myself. Or cut out my tongue."

"Okay," he said.

"Okay, I should shoot myself? Or okay, I can buy you a coffee?"

"No. And then yes."

"No, and then yes," she repeated. "Right." She adjusted her backpack on her shoulders. "Do you want to meet out-side or—"

"Outside," he said. He nodded several times. His hair flopped over his eyes. "Yeah. Outside."

The bell rang. They parted. She had calculus next. She somehow got through the rest of the day, wondering all the while if she had dreamed that conversation, imagined it, like imagining herself leaping on him. But, no, she had done it. Taken drastic action. And he was going to meet her. *Hooray*, she wanted to shout then. *Hooray! Hooray for me.* But at once she began to believe she had cornered him—she had!—and he had said yes because it was the easy thing to do. Anyway, *can I buy you a coffee*—what kind of invitation was that? A cheap one. Horrible! And in this way she tortured herself for the rest of the day.

After school he was waiting for her, leaning against a tree, one foot up, and he was chewing on a toothpick and looked adorable. He's there, she thought. He's there because of me. She wanted to shout or sing or wave her arms around. Then she saw that he looked frightened. Of her? But he was a *boy*.

"Hey," she said, coming up to him.

"Hey."

"We're going . . . to get coffee," she said. "Right?"

"I guess."

They walked down the street, came to the corner, crossed, walked down the next block. Neither said anything. Another block. Silence. And another. And more silence. Silence building like stones.

"Over there," Beauty said finally, pointing with relief to Clara's Coffee Shoppe on a small strip mall. He nodded.

They crossed the street, and she could have walked into a speeding car without ever having seen it coming. She had no idea how she had crossed safely. And she had no idea who this boy was, why they were together, what she could ever find to say to him. Her teeth chattered.

"Cold?" he said.

"A little."

"H-h-h-here!" He pulled off his jacket, draped it over her shoulders.

"Oh," she breathed. "Thank you." The jacket held the warmth of his body, and she hoped never to give it back.

They entered the coffee shop, sat at the counter. "My treat." She tried to sound sure of herself. She pulled his jacket around her.

He ordered a large coffee, regular. She ordered a small coffee, vanilla flavored.

"F-f-f-flavored?" he said. "You like that? I say, never flavor coffee."

"Really?" They were talking now. She sat up straighter, sparkled her eyes at him, got bold and said teasingly, "Never flavor coffee! Okay. Why not?"

"Ruins the taste." He said it solemnly, so she answered in the same vein—serious, grave. "I'll never do it again."

"Good," he said. He smiled a little to himself, as if he was glad he had changed her mind. Then he looked at her and touched his jacket, and said, "Warm now?"

"Oh, yes!" she said, and got warmer, she was sure her cheeks were flushed. She put her hands to them. Yes, warm. "Do you want your jacket back?"

"Eventually, yes. Keep it on for now."

"Thank you!"

They smiled at each other and drank their coffee. He finished first and twirled on the stool. "Well, thanks," he said. And then he said her name. "Thanks, Beauty."

"Ethan, you're welcome." She paid, and they walked out together.

At the corner he said, "I go this way. See you around, I guess." He reddened. "I mean, I'll see you in h-h-history class t-t-t-tomorrow."

"Yes," she said, "see you there, for sure." She took off his jacket and handed it to him, watched as he put it on, warm from her now. And she hoped he would do something affectionate. Was holding her hand, even for a moment, too much to wish for? She would settle for a touch on her neck or her arm, any little gesture.

But they parted, and he walked away without looking

back. "'Bye," she called. Her voice lifted. "'Bye, Ethan." He kept walking.

She made herself turn and not look back. The ordeal, for surely it had been that, was over, and her legs were boneless with relief, but as she walked home, almost wobbly at first, she began singing a song she'd learned from her father a long time ago, when she was about Autumn's age. She'd heard him singing it for Autumn last summer, before he fell and stopped singing and speaking.

"'Four strong winds that blow lonely, seven seas that run high, all these things that won't change—'" She couldn't remember what came next. She hummed, found a few of the words: "'now, our good times are all gone—'" or was it "'our good times are just begun'"? She liked that better, sang it again, bravely, wanting to believe it. "'Our good times are just begun!'"

AN OLD-FASHIONED VIRTUE

"HELLO, GIRLS," the man says.

It's Sunday afternoon, and he's sitting on a bench in the park facing the duck pond. He has brought bread in a plastic bag for the ducks. The trees are leafing out, the sky is blue after days of clouds, and the girls are coming along the path through the woods. His heart quickens.

"Hello, girls," he says quietly. They don't appear to hear him. He throws a piece of bread to the ducks, and they gather, squawking for the morsel. The girls come closer.

He says it again. "Hello, girls."

"Hello!" Her Dimness says. "Are you feeding the ducks? I love ducks, they're so cute, I wish I had some ducks, but I can't because of where we live, and I can't have a dog because of allergies, and—"

"Come on, Fancy," Hair Girl says. "Don't bother the man."

"She's not bothering me," he says. He tosses another piece of bread into the water.

"Oh, oh, look at them. Autumn, look at them! Are they fighting?" Her Dimness squats down. "Don't fight, ducks, it's not nice, you can share the bread. Share! Why don't you share? Please, be nice."

"Would you like to feed the ducks?" The man holds out a piece of bread.

"No, thank you," Hair Girl says. "We have to go home now."

She's polite. He likes that.

"Fancy, come *on*," she says. "They're waiting for us." She puts her finger in her mouth and twirls her gum on her tongue. Pink gum, pink tongue.

"No, not yet, please," Her Dimness whines. "I want to feed the ducks. Please, please, Autumn my sister, I want to feed the ducks, I do, I do."

"Oh, let her feed them, Autumn," he says, very gently. He likes her name. He says it to himself. *Autumn*. The other one has a rather stupid name, which is, of course, fitting.

"Well . . ." Autumn frowns deliciously. Then she gives him a little what-can-you-do look, an adult-to-adult look, and says, "Oh, okay, Fancy, go on. But don't take forever," she adds in a motherly tone.

"Try not to give it all to them at once," he advises, handing Fancy a slice of bread. "Tear it into small pieces."

"I will, I will, oh thank you, you are so nice," she cries, and she rushes to the edge of the water and begins scattering bread, laughing as the ducks clamor. "Oh, look, the little one there isn't getting any," she says. "That poor little baby duck, oooh, he is so cute!"

"Your sister is enthusiastic," he says to Autumn. She nods. She's shy. A delightful, old-fashioned virtue, shyness.

He smiles at her, but not too much of a smile. He doesn't want to scare her. He's just sharing his amusement at her sister. His pulse beats in his throat. As if he's both himself and someone else watching him and the two girls, he wonders what's going to happen. If some event, some change, some turn of fortune is about to take place. His eyes go slightly out of focus, and there's a buzzing in his head, a pleasant sound, as of bees in flowers.

Autumn sits down on the other end of the bench and bends over to untie one of her sneakers. "I've got a stone in my shoe," she says.

He nods. "That can be annoying." From the corner of his eye, he watches as she shakes out the sneaker, then puts it on again and ties it. She puffs a little, charmingly, as if bending over is strenuous. Her hair falls around her face, and when she sits up, she tucks it back behind her ears. Every little movement she makes is delicious.

"Autumn my sister!" Fancy runs up with her awkward stride and whispers in Autumn's ear.

"Can't you hold it?" Autumn says. She glances at him.

"No!" Fancy shakes her head. "I have to go bad," she whispers loudly. "Can I go over there?" She points into the woods.

"Well . . . okay. Go behind a tree. Don't pee on your shoes." Again, she glances at him. Her cheeks are red. She stands up. "Hurry, though, we have to go home."

"Okay, I will, I'll be quick." Fancy runs up the path into the woods. The sun is going down. In a moment she disappears from sight.

So there they are, the two of them. He offers her a stick

of gum. She shakes her head. "Sure?" he says. "I have enough."

And just as with the bread, she hesitates, bites her lip, then nods. She reaches out and takes the gum. Her fingers brush against his.

That evening the man weeps. Sitting at the table by the window that looks out over the empty lot, with his supper before him—the tomato soup in a bowl, the slice of cheese on a plate next to the stack of crackers—the man weeps.

He weeps out of gratitude. Nothing happened. He hasn't done wrong.

He holds his head in his hands, sobs juddering through him.

After a while he gets up and bends over the sink, splashing his face with cold water. The cats are watching him. He nods to them, goes back to the table, and sits down. He's hungry now, really hungry! He eats with gusto, letting himself slurp the soup and fill his mouth with crackers. Everything tastes delicious! The memory of the girls in the park is delicious as well, and so is the wind blowing around the house.

He considers his good luck, his wonderful luck. To have found this house, with no neighbors, with waste fields on either side and across the street, with a landlord in another state, a landlord who asks nothing, just glad to have someone responsible keep the building repaired and clean. To have found a job where no one bothers him. To have his lovely birds—yes, lovely, all five of them, even the dim one, even the ugly one, lovely really. In his relief, he knows them all to be lovely, delightful. And then, to have escaped his worst self, the self he works so hard to keep under control. Luck had been on his side. Just as Autumn took the gum, Her Dimness had come prancing out of the woods. A moment later the two of them had gone off together. Oh, yes, luck was his.

Afterward he takes both cats onto his lap and allows them to stay there while he sits in his living room like any other man, drinking a beer and watching TV.

THE RIGHTEOUS PATH

OVER THE WEEKEND her mother elected
Beauty to break the news to her sisters, news that she
alone had been entrusted with, so far. "No, you're not
going to do that," Beauty said.

"Yes, we are." Her mother blinked hard and screwed
her cigarette into the chipped dish she favored as an ashtray. "You tell them for me, honey. Please."

Beauty put off the unwelcome task until Sunday night.
After supper and an hour of watching a show, she told her
sisters to come up to her room. "Why?" Stevie said. "I've
got better things to do."

"You need to come up," Beauty said, and she gazed at

Stevie, hoping her face showed nothing but resolve. She went ahead up the attic stairs to wait for them. In her room she paced. She had been put on the spot by her parents. Nothing out of the ordinary in that. The oldest, the most responsible—who else could tell her sisters as well as she? Not their father. Too rough in his ways. Mimicking a famous saying, he had answered her protests with "I am the decider." But what about her mother, that tender heart? She had begged off, her cheeks ashen and sagging as she said, "Oh, no, honey! I can't do it, I just can't. You know me, I'll be crying my head off, I won't be any use at all."

"What's up?" Mim said. She was lying on her bed, next to the window, with a book perched on her stomach. She peered at Beauty nearsightedly.

Beauty shook her head. "Wait. Anyway, here they come."

Stevie was in the lead, her steps quick and firm. Behind her, Fancy toe tapping on each step, and bringing up the rear, Autumn patiently following Fancy. All of them were talking at full volume as they squirmed their way around the room and settled down.

Fancy seated herself on the floor, her legs crossed, her

knees touching the ground. Fancy was flexible in a way Beauty envied, but what in the world was the child wearing? One of her odd getups: a tiny pink shortie top that Beauty recognized as a Stevie castoff, a ruffled orange skirt that her mother had discarded after spilling bleach on it, way too big for Fancy but gathered together with a safety pin, and on her head a red paper crown.

Autumn and Stevie collapsed on Beauty's bed, under the eaves, bickering over a pair of Stevie's jeans that Autumn had borrowed to wear to school ". . . without permission," Stevie said, her voice just short of a shout. "And you're way, way too big for them. You've probably stretched them all out of size."

"I did not. Anyway, I'm the same size as you."

"Okay, quiet down," Beauty said, but they didn't.

"The same size? Oh, please! Look at your legs and look at mine." Stevie stuck out her legs and pulled up her jeans. "Your legs are much fatter."

Autumn twirled her hair furiously. "I do not have fat legs. You shouldn't say such a thing."

"Oh, well, if you want to believe that, what do I care. But we're not the same size, not for a moment." Stevie put her hands around her little waist and looked pointedly at her breasts, which were not little. Autumn had no breasts yet, to speak of, and not much of a waist, either. "Anyway, we don't have to talk about it," Stevie said. She smiled condescendingly. "You can't borrow my clothes without permission. Got that? End of discussion."

"Why are you so fussy and selfish?" Autumn wailed. "I only wore them for one day."

"Don't fight, you two, bad two." Fancy spit on her fingers and clapped her hands in some obscure ritual of her own. "Don't fight, ain't right, tonight I'll fly a kite, that's a poem, that's a good poem, I'll tell Mrs. Sokolow my teacher tomorrow, she likes my poems."

But there was no stopping Stevie. She was on the righteous path. "They're my pants, Autumn, and I am not selfish. Take that back! I just want my things left alone. I don't want other people messing around with them."

"I'm not other people," Autumn wept. "I'm your sister."

"You two," Beauty said, "you two oil and water people, stop now, I have something to tell you, all of you." She spoke too quietly. Quiet did not prevail.

Stevie's rational tone had evaporated, and she was talking loudly into Autumn's ear, while Fancy had picked up on "oil and water people" and was repeating it over and over with pleasure. It was a madhouse.

Standing near the bureau, fingering the scarf draped around her shoulders, Beauty was ready to just give up, quit trying to quiet them down. She didn't want to deliver this message, anyway. "Be quiet," she said again, and finally raised her voice. "All right, then, shut up. I have to tell you all something. And it's important. So shut *up*."

Beauty's stomach heaved. All eyes were trained on her now. Mim nodded slightly, as if she knew it wasn't going to be good, while Stevie pursed her lips suspiciously and Autumn's eyes went out of focus. Only Fancy went on chanting, "Oil and water people," mesmerizing herself. Mim ran two fingers across Fancy's mouth in the zipper motion.

Beauty pulled the ends of the scarf together, then in a sudden flush of heat said rapidly, "You know what a hard time Mommy and Poppy . . ." She faltered. Why was she using those childish names? Only Autumn, the baby of the family, and Fancy, who might as well have been the baby, called their parents by those names. "They're having, I mean, we're all having, we're a family, it's all of us—"

What a botch of a job she was doing. She straightened her shoulders and began again. "You guys know Auntie

Bernice is all alone over there in New Hampshire, and she's lonely, and she could use some help, and things are tough here with money, you know, so Mom and Dad have decided—" She took a breath. "They've decided to lend Stevie to Auntie Bernie for a while, just to ease things up here. Auntie Bernie's happy about it. She'll pay Stevie's dental bills, which are big. Huge. Right, Stevie? And she'll give you an allowance and money for clothes for helping her around the house," she said, watching Stevie. "It's not forever," she added.

"They're going to *lend* me?" Stevie said, in a choked, low voice.

"Me," Fancy said. "Me. Lend me. I want to live with Auntie Bernie."

Mim stood up, as if they were at a meeting. "Lend Stevie?" Her voice, unusually, was loud. "What is she, a sack of groceries? A cup of sugar? A pair of shoes?" Her voice rose even louder. "That's *disgusting*."

Beauty cleared her throat. "Since Dad fell off the roof at the Lesley place and has been laid up, not able to work—"

"What's that got to do with lending me?" Stevie said, her hand across her mouth.

"It's money," Beauty said. "Yeah, money. That's what it's all about." Beauty saw that she was wringing her hands, something she thought took place only in books. She stared at her hands for a moment and then, with an effort, pulled them apart and clasped them behind her back.

"Whose idea was this?" Mim asked.

Beauty shook her head. "Don't, Mim," she pleaded. "Don't go there."

"Don't? Don't ask? I think Stevie deserves the truth."

"Yes, I do. Whose idea was it?" Stevie said, and the strange thing was that she, the shouter of the family, seemed to have changed places—or voices, anyway—with Mim. She was the one now speaking softly. "I want to know."

"Dad's, I think," Beauty said reluctantly.

"Figures." Stevie gave a small laugh. "And Mom is such a sap, she does anything he says."

"Isn't that child abuse, lending out one of your kids?" Autumn said. She started sobbing. "I bet they could be arrested or something."

"Oh, no," Fancy cried. "I don't want to go to jail."

"Everybody, quiet. Fancy, you're not going to jail," Beauty said. "Nobody's going to jail. Listen," she said to them all, "I'm trying to explain."

"Oh, the hell you are." Stevie leaped to her feet. Gone was the small Mim-ish voice. "I should punch you out," she said, as if the whole thing were Beauty's idea, had nothing to do with their parents. "You always wanted to get rid of me, and I know why."

"Honey," Beauty said.

"I'm prettier than you. I'm the pretty one," Stevie said. "And I have a boyfriend. And you—can't—stand—it." Her face was bright with fury or fear. Her hair stood out all around her head, crackled as if struck with lightning.

"Honey," Beauty repeated helplessly, and began to cry.

EVERYBODY IN THE WORLD CRIED

MY FACE IS HOT, it is *sooo* hot, maybe I will die with hotness. I have The Urge, like Beauty my sister told me about, so I am hot and talking, but nobody is listening, and my face is stiff like paper, because I cried. First Beauty my sister cried. No, first she said Mommy was going to lend Stevie my sister. And then she cried. And then I cried. Stevie my sister is mean to me, but I don't want her lended out.

And Autumn my sister cried. She leaned her head on my shoulder and she said Fancy, Fancy, she said my name like that, Fancy, Fancy, Fancy, and I cried more and more and more. And I think everybody in the world cried, only

Mim my sister didn't cry, she said crying won't do any good, because I never saw Mim my sister cry, not ever, but just sometimes, because she is not a crying person like me and Autumn.

And then Mommy came up the stairs, and she said, Oh, that is so hard to climb, and she was making big breaths, and she wanted to hug Stevie my sister, but she said No, don't you hug me, I hate you. And then Mommy cried. And I wanted to stop crying. But I didn't.

And then Poppy came up the stairs on his crutches, and I could hear him bang, bang up the stairs, and he said, "What is going on here?" And we all cried some more, and we were saying not to lend Stevie my sister to anybody, not even Auntie Bernie, and Poppy said, "Well, girls, we have to do it and if I could loan you all out I would do it in a heartbeat," and he said that was because we're not having any money. Then he said something really funny. He said, "When my ship comes in, we won't have anything to worry about." But isn't that funny? Because he has no ships.

And then Beauty my sister said she would get more work on her job and give all the money to Poppy and ride her bike to work in the mall two miles away and not take the car or the bus to save money. And Poppy said it was all talk and no money, and his back hurt bad from the stairs and we would lend Stevie my sister to Auntie Bernie, anyway, until he got better and suddenly, guess what, the lights went out, all the lights were dark, and it was scary and we all screamed, and Poppy said a really bad curse word that begins with *F* that you're not supposed to say, and he said that word three times.

And Mommy said it must be a power outage or maybe it's Mr. God or maybe it isn't, and she said, "Huddle Herbert, did you pay the electric bill?" and he said "With what, Blossom?" and it was dark, and they weren't nice to each other. So I cried more.

GATE IN HER THROAT

STANDING IN THE lunch line, Beauty was jolted by a kick to her heel. "That's my foot, jerk!" she snapped, and she turned to see Ethan smiling at her. "Was that supposed to be a new kind of greeting?" She meant it to be funny, but it came out sullen.

The smile faded. "Whoa," Ethan said, putting up his hands. "What's b-b-b-biting you?"

"Nothing," she said, pushing her lunch tray along the metal bars. How could she explain her hideous mood without telling him everything—the stupid news about lending Stevie and how, all week, she had been running from sister to sister, wiping tears, soothing tempers, excusing what she didn't want to excuse. Could she say that a moment ago it had just felt *good* to give in and snap at someone, to let herself go, to lose it?

She took a can of soda and turned to say she was sorry. The least she could do. But Ethan was gone, moving through the crowded cafeteria, his shoulders hunched so tightly they were practically up around his ears. So *she* was the jerk. She'd just ruined everything. He was sensitive—didn't she know that about him already?

She grabbed her tray, paid, and left the line. Ethan was slouched at one of the small tables all the way across the room, near the door. She wanted to go to him, and she didn't dare. She sat down at the edge of a bench, next to a girl she knew from math class. "Hey, Beauty," Ruby said.

"Hey, Ruby." She stared at the bowl of soup on her tray, dipped in her spoon, and left it there. She wasn't hungry. Her father thought they were going to save money by sending Stevie away. One less mouth to feed, etcetera. Beauty had tried talking to her father, persuading him that it wasn't worth making everyone miserable, but he stonewalled her. "I've made up my mind." He was like a horse with blinders. He was desperate to do *something* to help out the family, and that was all he could see.

She glanced at the clock. In ten minutes the bell would ring. Ethan was still at the table in the far corner, still alone. She stood up. Go over to him, she told herself. Do it, you'll think of something to say. Her stomach thudding, she picked up her tray and threaded her way through the tables, returning greetings, nodding to all these people she had known for years, some of them since kindergarten.

"Hey, Marsha . . . Dyane . . . Kerry . . ." The little smile, the quick lift of the voice. Did they know she and Ethan Boswell were—well, whatever they were, if they were anything, anymore. Of course, they knew. They knew everything, saw everything, talked about everything. This was *Mallory*.

She stopped at Ethan's table, stood next to him. "Ethan?" He didn't look up. He shoved his hand into a bag of chips, brought out a bunch, and poked them into his mouth. He chewed, showing teeth, tongue, the mashed-up chips.

"Ethan?" she said again.

"Yeah? What?"

She put her tray on the table, sat down across from him, and picked up her can of soda. A sip of liquid squeaked past the gate in her throat. "I'm sorry." Another sip. Her lips were like clay. "I'm—I've got . . . things on my mind, and—"

"Yeah. Sure," he said. "Forget it."

"No, Ethan. It's like this—"

"I didn't kill you, you know," he said. "I just sort of—"

"I know," she said. "It didn't even hurt, really. It's just—there's a mess at home," she blurted. "A mess, and I'm freaked, and I acted stupid. I'm sorry. Hello. Can you say something, please."

"Yeah, you did act s-s-stupid."

"Thank you."

They looked at each other, smiled sheepishly.

"So, let's pretend we're back in the line," she said, almost happy again. "You just kicked my foot. I turn around and say, 'Ethan! Hi!' And you say—"

He cleared his throat. "Uh. Hi."

"And then we walk over to this table together, and—"

"You want to see a m-m-m movie?" he interrupted, getting the words out quickly. "*History of Violence*. I was going to ask you."

"History of what?" Maybe she heard him wrong. Maybe it was *valence*, a movie about curtains.

"Violence. History of."

"Right, that's what I thought you said. So it's educational?"

"No. It's not. No education. No school. Worry not."

"If you say so. When and where?"

"Saturday night. My house."

Nathan, the New Hampshire cousin, was due to show up Saturday. Her sisters, Stevie especially, would need her to be there. "I can't," she said.

He pulled at an earring. Was that surprise she saw on his face? "How about Friday night?"

Oh, let me think. Can I possibly be free? Yes. How unusual! "What time?"

"Seven, seven thirty?"

Friday she worked four to six. Maybe Patrick would let her off work early. He would. He was good about things like that.

"I'll pick you up," Ethan said.

"You have a driver's license?"

"Uh-huh, don't you?"

"No, not yet."

"You should get it. Around q-q-quarter after seven, okay?"

That would leave her just about enough time to get home, shower, change her clothes, and eat something. She'd wait outside for him. One thing she wasn't going to do was bring him anywhere near the squall that was her family right now.

A NIGHT AT THE MOVIES

"WE HAD TO MOVE everything in this room every which way after we got that," Ethan's mother said proudly, ushering Beauty into the living room. She didn't identify "that," but she didn't have to. The huge, curved plasma screen, hanging on the wall over the fireplace, loomed over the furniture, the rugs, the windows—everything, in fact, including the Boswell parents, Ethan, and Beauty—like a strange god arrived from outer space. "But we do love it," Mrs. Boswell said, giving the screen a fond pat, as if it were a new and favorite pet.

Beauty glanced at Ethan. In this brand-new social situation, she was unsure how to respond. Politely? *I'm really*

125

sorry that you had to do all that work. Enthusiastically? *It's fabulous! You are so lucky!* Or truthfully? *That screen would make ten of our TVs, and it's actually pretty ugly.*

She settled for smiling and nodding, and hoping fervently that Mr. Boswell, who had seated himself on the couch facing the screen, would now rise and say to Mrs. Boswell, "Come on, let's leave the kids alone." That would be perfect.

But no. It didn't look as if they were going anywhere soon. Mrs. Boswell took the other end of the couch, patted the cushion in the middle, and beckoned Beauty to sit down. Then she patted Beauty on the knee (her third pat in the last three minutes) and said, "We're so pleased Ethan has a new friend."

Beauty blinked. So! She was a *new* friend. The ugly little dog named jealousy woke up and barked. *Who's the old friend? What's her name? Is she pretty? Where is she now?* Ethan, who had said nothing this whole time, blushed at his mother's remark. He was sitting to the left of his father in an upholstered armchair, patterned with tiny roses, and his whole face turned pretty much the same color red.

"Okay, folks, settle down, settle in," Mr. Boswell said.

126

"The movie's going to begin." He aimed the remote.

"Hey, Mom," Ethan said, finally finding his voice.

Beauty shot him an encouraging look with a message. *Right! Ask her to change seats with you.* Although neither of them had said it in so many words, hadn't they intended to sit together *and* as close as possible, while watching the movie?

"Mom, what about—"

"Quiet, please," his father said, nicely enough. "We all want to watch the movie."

So the movie started, and Beauty sat pinned between the Boswells, while Ethan, alone in the armchair, which could have nicely held the two of them, leaned forward, ever more absorbed by the action on the screen. Did he even know anymore that she was in the room?

Later, while he was driving her home, they didn't exactly have a fight, but the evening ended badly. They talked about the movie, which Beauty hadn't really liked— maybe that put a bit of chill in the air; the movie had been Ethan's choice, after all. Even so, they might have got past it, but then she said, "It's weird the way your parents stuck to us." And when he didn't respond, she added,

"Like glue. Elmer's glue."

"I don't want to talk about them," he said, and the air got a little chillier.

They rode the rest of the way to her house in silence. There was a moment after he parked when they looked at each other, and there might have been a kiss. She leaned a little toward him, then he said, "Well, see ya," and looked straight ahead.

She nodded and pushed open the door. "Thanks," she said automatically. "Nice time." She walked toward the house. Behind her, she heard the car pull away.

THE KIDNAPPER

SATURDAY MORNING you're watching out your bedroom window when a red pickup truck stops in front of the house, and the kidnapper emerges. A short, compact man, he looks up and down the street. He's wearing jeans and a tight black T-shirt. He yawns and stretches, lifting his arms and rotating his shoulders.

You're leaning on your elbows, your chin in your hands, and you stare at him and stare at him. You see that his arms have lots of muscles. You see that his black hair is slicked back and shiny, and even from up here you can see the dimple in his chin. Maybe some people would think he's handsome, maybe you even think so, but you hate him, anyway, because that's *him*, the Nathan cousin from New Hampshire, the one who's going to take away Stevie, but still you're a little bit proud that you're the first one in the family to see him.

Fancy crowds you aside, so she can see out the window, too. "Who is that boy, who is he? Oooh, oooh, he's pretty."

"Boys aren't pretty," you say.

"Oh, I love him, he's so pretty, look at his hair. I'm going to marry him and have babies."

"Stop being stupid," you say. "You're not going to marry anybody."

"Liar, liar, pants on fire, I am too going to marry some-body," Fancy says. "This lady came and said we have to learn about marrying and kisses and things like that, because we are same as everyone like about love and stuff, but we don't want to get in trouble, so we have to learn things about boyfriends and be super-super-super-duper careful."

You watch as the cousin reaches into the truck and pulls out a duffle bag. He slings it over his shoulder, and then, as if he knows you're up there spying on him, he tilts his head back and looks right up at you, *and he waves.*

You want to duck or fall down or something, but Fancy

is still talking in your ear, and then she says, "Are you listening to me?" And she pinches you on the arm.

Your eyes fill with tears, even though it wasn't a really hard pinch, and you wish that Mommy's cousin would get back in his truck, get in there *right now* and drive away and never come back. It's true that sometimes you hate Stevie so much that you make up stories in your mind where she falls into the river or gets lost in the woods or smooshed by one of the big trucks carrying logs, but you always make the stories turn out happy. You're the one who pulls her out of the river, you find her in the woods, you save her just before the truck runs her over. And you never, ever lend her out.

No matter what Mommy says about Stevie going to New Hampshire, or how Poppy tries to make it sound like something good, the way you think of it, Nathan Menand is here to *kidnap* Stevie, to take her away to New Hampshire, and who knows if you'll ever see her again.

THINGS SHE DIDN'T KNOW

"MIM," BEAUTY SAID. "Mim? Hello?"

Her sister, asleep in the next bed, shifted slightly, only her neat profile showing above the quilt pulled up around her head. Beauty watched her, willing her awake. The waxing moon, almost full, shone brilliantly through the window, and by its light she checked the time on the little clock near her bed. Two A.M. It was already Sunday. She had shut off the light around eleven last night, or was it closer to midnight? Whatever, she hadn't been able to sleep for thinking about her *object of desire*, Cousin Nathan.

She had almost lost the power of speech when she met

him. It was that gaze he turned on her, as if he was seeing the *real* Beauty, the one inside her skin. He had held her hand in his paw—big hands for a small man—for a long moment, then nodded as if he knew something about her that no one else knew. And it happened again. She fell! Or maybe it was Nathan who fell—into the space in her heart vacated by Ethan.

Wasn't it wild! Only a few days ago, she'd had this mammoth crush on Ethan, and now it was Nathan. Maybe not so wild. Those fifteen minutes in Ethan's car Friday night after the movie had flattened her. That painful moment when he could have kissed her—and, instead, had turned away—had restored her to her senses, to her sense of who she was . . . and who she wasn't.

Supposing Nathan—*Cousin* Nathan, she reminded herself, tucking her hands between her thighs—supposing he decided to stay for a few more days? Supposing he liked her? *Loved* her. He had worked, traveled, seen things, been places—all the things she longed for, for herself. He was older, but she didn't care. He was her cousin, but she didn't care about that, either, or that he'd be gone tomorrow morning. It was all fantasy, anyway, which was the history of her life. She must have made some sound.

Mim woke up. "Beauty," she said. "Are you okay?"

"Yeah, I'm just crazy tonight. Go back to sleep."

Mim yawned. "What time is it?"

"About two."

Mim reached for the bottle of water she kept on the floor. "Wow, look at the moon."

"I know, it's beautiful. Mim . . . do you have a boyfriend?"

"You know I don't." She yawned again.

"But you're so cute, I bet there are plenty of boys who—"

"Maybe, but I'm not interested."

How was that possible? Beauty was interested; she'd always been interested. She'd been thinking about boys, looking at them, in love with them, since she was six years old. "There's no one you especially like, no, uh, *object of desire*?"

"Object of desire." Mim laughed and pulled the quilt around her shoulders. "I didn't say that."

Ah, that was better. "Would you tell him? I mean, would you, uh, declare yourself to him?"

"Declare myself—maybe. What about you?"

"I have, once. And now I—hmm, I—oh, well . . ." She wasn't quite ready to confess. "Would you not do it, Mim, because girls don't? Or shouldn't? Or because you're too shy—"

"No, no, and no. If I wanted to, if I thought the time was right or something like that, I would."

"Then why don't you?"

"I have my reasons."

"Is he too old?" Now Beauty approached the subject she really wanted to talk about.

"No."

"Is he unavailable for other reasons?"

"Yes and no."

"What does that mean?"

"It means, I would tell her if I thought she felt the same way."

"Her?" Beauty said. "Oh. *Her*."

"Yes."

"Then you're—"

"Yes."

"Oh." Beauty lay back on the bed, her hands on top of her head, Nathan forgotten, as she took in this new information, took in how ignorant she had been of Mim's real self. It had never occurred to her that there were things she didn't know about her sisters.

"Well," she said finally. "Okay. So, who is she?"

"It's just someone . . . someone in school."

"Do I know her?"

"Maybe."

"Is she, uh, like, uh—"

Mim reached between the beds and shook Beauty's arm. "You can say the L word. It won't burn your tongue. Yes, I think she is. Beauty, you won't tell anyone—especially not Mom and Dad. I'm not ashamed or anything, but here—Mallory, you know what I mean."

"Do you love her?"

"I think so."

"How do you know? How do you know it's the real thing? I get these crushes . . ."

Mim hunched over her knees. "The real thing—what is that, anyway? Maybe I'm just wishing it is, because . . . it's lonely—" Her voice caught.

Beauty pushed aside her covers and went to sit beside Mim. She had so many little sisters and the other three took so much attention that she often just forgot about Mim. She was the one who always seemed okay, but now here she sat, her knees up defensively.

"Are you sad, honey?"

"Not just for me. It's Stevie. It's the worst thing that ever happened in our family. Dad is so—"

"Stubborn," Beauty supplied. "He's a mule. Stevie's kind of a pain in the butt for everybody, but she's our *sister*." She sighed. "And now, you and I, we're both in unrequited love."

"You, too?" Mim said, and she sounded a little surprised.

"Well, not with a girl."

"Oh," Mim said. "Oh, okay."

"I think we should just have a big crying jag and get it over with."

"Waaaa!" Mim mocked, and they both laughed.

It was the next day when they cried. Cried harder than they'd ever cried in their lives.

COUSIN DARLIN'

SUNDAYS, BEAUTY WAS in the habit of giving her mother a break from the cooking. So midmorning, she was at the stove, making pancakes for the family brunch, when Nathan came dancing into the kitchen. She smelled him before she saw him, that strong, beautiful man-smell of sweat. She turned to look at him. He was glowing, raising his arms and dancing triumphantly. "I had me a run. Five miles, folks."

Beauty's father, who was sitting at the table repairing a toaster, made a barking sound. "You're too skinny."

Their first amiable meeting had not let down deep roots. Although Huddle had called this whole scenario into being, he seemed to resent Nathan's presence, but Nathan either didn't notice or didn't care. Or, Beauty thought, he was one damn good actor, but didn't care was her guess.

"When are you going to start running, Beauty?" Nathan said.

"Oh, I don't know." She turned back to the stove and flipped a pancake onto the stack she intended to keep warm in the oven. "Maybe pretty soon I'll start," she added untruthfully.

"How about tomorrow morning?"

She shook her head. "Tomorrow morning won't be good. I have to go, uh, somewhere." She didn't want to say *school*, didn't want him to think of her that way, as a schoolgirl. She stirred the pancake mix furiously. Stupid of her.

"Where'd you get that toaster, Poppy?" Nathan bent over Huddle's shoulder. Within the first hour of arriving, Nathan had taken up Autumn and Fancy's names for their parents as if he were one of the kids. Beauty glanced at him. He was almost the same age as her mother.

"That toaster is a little beauty," he said admiringly, and gave Beauty a quick look.

"It's the old-fashioned kind," Beauty said, flushing.

"That's right," he said, "two slots for bread and no other functions."

"Got it in a thrift shop," Beauty's father said without looking up. His tools were scattered all over the table—the screwdrivers, a utility knife, a roll of colored tape, and a loop of copper wire. "Three bucks," he said, "and it works like a charm. I just have to replace the cord. Then I can sell it for seven, eight dollars."

Nathan nodded. "Nice, very nice. You're a thinking man. It's great to have your own business, isn't it? I'm still working for someone else."

"Something's burning," her mother yelled from the back shed, where she was hanging laundry on the clothes rack. "Beauty. What's burning?"

"Nothing, Mom. It's all right." She turned the fire down under the pancake grill. In fact, the pancake in the middle of the grill was singed around the edges. Nathan reached around Beauty and took one off the stack. "Wait. I'm going to warm them," she said.

"I know that, cousin, darlin'," he said, "but I'm so hungry, I could take a bite out of you."

She blushed again, but said, briskly, as if she couldn't

140

feel the heat of him behind her, "Get yourself a slice of bread."

"Will do," he said, and moved away.

She grabbed her stirring hand by the wrist to keep it from shaking and stirred the remainder of the pancake batter long past the moment when she could have stopped.

RUNNING AWAY TO FLORIDA

LYING ON YOUR bed, you're reading a comic book, waiting for the pancakes to be ready, and trying as hard as you can to ignore Stevie, who's on her bunk bed above you, being really noisy, making all kinds of grunts and groans and weird sounds, bouncing around from one side of the bed to the other. You could get out your bike and take a ride, but you're *chillin'*, like Stevie says when she's in a good mood, which is definitely not today, because she's so freaked about going away tomorrow morning.

You *totally* understand. You're not in a good mood, either, sort of for the same reason. Last night the loud voices downstairs, where your parents were arguing and talking and going on about Stevie and money and jobs and other stuff like that, kept you awake for *hours*. When you couldn't stand it anymore, you went downstairs and stood in the kitchen doorway, where they could see you, and said, "Hey." But no one even noticed you were there. "Hey," you said again, and they still didn't notice you, so you went back to bed, but you didn't fall asleep right away, and that's why you're a little cranky right now.

Stevie is kicking her legs so hard on the mattress, you think she's going to kick right through it and land on top of you. "Hey," you say. You don't say it in a mean, mad way, like you said last night to the grown-ups, you say it just nice, but she doesn't answer. So you say it again, louder. "Hey, Stevie?" You know she heard you, because she kicks even harder, but she still doesn't answer. Kicking is so ridiculous! She's fourteen years old, she shouldn't be kicking like a baby. Still, you'd be mad, too, if Mommy and Poppy were lending you to someone. You don't think they ever would do that, because you're the youngest and, like your sisters are always saying, sort of spoiled and Mommy's favorite.

But then something occurs to you. How can you be

143

positive that they would never lend you away? Maybe they would do it. Poppy said it, didn't he? He said—and now you think for a moment, and then you've got it. He said he'd lend *all* of you, if he got half a chance. He didn't say he'd lend all of you *except Autumn*.

Thinking about this gives your stomach that cold, nasty feeling, like the times in the car when you think you're going to throw up, but you don't, and then it's even worse than if you did throw up and got it over with. You sit up and, all at once, your eyes are wet and your throat is tight, and you think you're going to start crying right then and there. "Stevie," you say, but before you can get another word out, Stevie yells, "Don't say my name. I didn't give you permission."

You feel like yelling at her that she's mean and selfish, but then you see the duffle bag on the floor, stuffed with all her clothes and earrings and her elephant with one ear that she sleeps with, and you think how this is going to be the last night for a long, long time that she'll be sleeping in the bunk bed over you. And that makes you be like Stevie and hate them all. You wish you could wash out their mouths with soap, like Mommy is always saying she'll do to you if you say the F-word or the A-word.

144

"Hey, Stevie," you say, "I don't want you to go away with Cousin Nathan. I'll miss you too much."

For a moment she stops thrashing, like she's thinking about what you said. Then she leans over the side of the bed and says, as mean as mean can be, "Shut up, and don't talk to me."

"It's not me," you say. "I'm not sending you away, I'm not lending you."

"I told you, *shut up*," she says in a weird voice, "I hate you all," and you wonder if she's going to cry. She never cries. She's always calling you a crybaby, snivel-snot nose, and other names like that. You thump your legs. She doesn't even care that you said something nice to her. You're mad! And sort of mixed up, too, sort of crazy feeling. It makes you want to scratch your face all over, but if you do that, Mommy will yell at you that you're ruining your beautiful skin.

You don't know what to do, so you get up and go outside, and you *still* don't know what to do. You think about going back in and eating pancakes, which should be ready pretty soon, but you're just too mad at everybody, so you start walking, and you think about running away from home. Maybe you and Stevie could run away to Florida or

145

someplace nice like that, and she wouldn't have to go to New Hampshire, and she'd probably love you a lot for saving her.

You walk for a long time, making up the story about going to Florida with Stevie, and after a while you look around, and you're on a street you don't know. It's called Elm Street, and it's mostly just houses like your street, but not as many, and you keep walking, and then you're on another street, you didn't notice the name or maybe there isn't even a street sign. There're only a couple of houses way down on the other end of the street, and everything else is mostly bushes and trash and junk. Well, not really junk—*weeds*, which aren't really bad things, like some people think. Poppy taught you the names of a lot of weeds, not just dandelions, which everyone knows. He taught you mustard and wild onion and that tall one with the reddish kind of leaves called dock, and Japanese knotweed, and he said you could eat a lot of that stuff in the springtime, including dandelion leaves.

You decide to spell *dandelion*. Mim told you to try spelling all the hard words. She said if you do that, after a while, it gets lots easier. So you stop walking to concentrate, and you say, "Dandelion. *D-A-N-D-A-L-I-O-N.*"

Wait. Is it an *A* or an *E* after the dand part? You try again. "Dandelion. *D-A-N-D-E-L-I-O-N*." Both ways sound right to you. Rats! You don't want to think about it anymore.

You squat down in the empty field and you hug your knees and look at the things that are growing right along with all the trash, the beer bottles and the sticky papers and some awful reddish gloop, which you don't even want to know what it is. You squat there for a while, watching a bunch of ants rushing around, and thinking that when Poppy is feeling good again, he'll show you more stuff about nature and plants. He could spell *dandelion* for you, too.

It's getting sort of windy, though, and a little bit dark in the sky, like it might rain, and now you notice that you're hungry, really hungry. It must be way past Sunday brunch time. You missed the pancakes, and now you're sorry, and you're ready to go home, but you've lost track of the streets. You're not exactly lost, but you're not exactly sure how to get home, either. You need to ask somebody.

You stand up and brush off your jeans and look around. You better go to one of those houses down on the other end of the street. Oh, lucky you! Someone is out in front of the first house, raking. You walk toward the house, humming to yourself, because you don't want the man to think you're scared of being lost or anything like that. He's raking old dried leaves into a big pile, and you think about jumping in leaves and how much fun that is, but you usually do that in the fall, not in the spring. The man doesn't seem to notice that you're coming along, so you walk right up to him and say in your politest voice, "Hello. Could you tell me something, please?"

BURNED PANCAKES

EVEN THOUGH THE sky had darkened, and it looked like it might rain, Beauty opened a window to clear out the smoke from the burned pancakes, which were Nathan's fault. Well, not really. She'd been distracted by him, the way he wiped his face with his sweatshirt, showing his belly, small, hard, smooth, like an orange. What would it be like to touch that belly, to put her hand over it?

Fancy brought her sewing into the kitchen and sat down. "Stinks in here," she said cheerfully, laying her head on their father's shoulder. He patted her and went on sorting nails and screws into separate piles. Nathan was sitting next to him, watching and occasionally picking up a nail and putting it in the right box. A wave of pity for her father went through Beauty. He looked so old and white, so thin shouldered, next to Nathan, whose skin almost glowed with health.

Her mother came into the kitchen and sat down at the table, but immediately jumped up, saying, "I should change this shirt. It smells like a cafeteria."

"Smells like a cafeteria?" Fancy repeated in her fast, high voice. "That is a funny joke, Mommy! Smells like a cafeteria," she said again, her voice parading over the words.

Nathan leaned and sniffed her mother's neck. "Smells good to me."

What a jerk, Beauty thought unwillingly. Flirting with her mother? Her father was watching, too. Beauty thought she might just strangle her so-called *object of desire*. She leaned over the table toward her father. "Dad, we really need to clean up here. Can I help you do that?"

"I'm good," he said, and gathered up his tools and the thin strands of copper wire.

Beauty closed the window again and went to the staircase. "Mim," she called, "are you going to set the table, or do you want me to do it?" She waited, her hand on the banister. This was usually Stevie's job, but Beauty wasn't about to ask her for anything today. Poor kid, being sent away. No matter how much Stevie raged or how much people bickered with each other, they were family—that was the bottom line.

"I'll do it, Beauty," Mim answered.

In the kitchen her father cleared away his tools and his toolbox. Mim set the table. Her mother appeared in a fresh blouse. Stevie came in, looking at no one and, the only one who didn't like pancakes, poured herself a bowl of cold cereal. So they were all there, all except Autumn, who was probably outside, playing somewhere. Beauty dropped more batter on the pan, then sat down. The sausages were passed around, then the pancakes.

"Hey, terrific," Nathan said, chewing. "Your daughter's a good cook, Poppy."

The pancake platter went around again. Nathan asked for more coffee, and Beauty poured for him and for her father.

"Where is that girl, anyway?" her mother said. She put the clean knife and fork on Autumn's plate and looked at Beauty. "Save your sister some pancakes. I don't think she ate anything this morning." Her mother put her hands to her face and pushed at her cheeks. She always did that when she was anxious or worried.

"Now don't get yourself all fretted up," Beauty's father said. He clanked down his coffee cup. "You hear me, Blossom? A few hours without food ain't going to hurt her. She'll show up when she gets hungry."

Beauty's mother nodded. "I know. I just can't help worrying."

"Worry bug," Fancy said brightly. "You're a big worry bug, Mommy."

MAPS

THE MAN STOPS raking the leaves and looks up, sort of startled. "Hello," he says, and that's when you recognize him. It's that nice man from the duck pond, the one who gave you the gum, which of course you shouldn't have taken from a stranger, but he was all right, he just gave you the gum and then when Fancy came back from peeing in the woods, he said good-bye and left.

You're pretty sure he doesn't recognize you. Why would he? You're just a kid and you're too shy to say about seeing him before. You ask him if he knows the best way for you to go home. "I live on Carbon Street," you say.

He straightens up and repeats slowly, "Carbon Street,"

153

like he's thinking about it, about the best way to tell you to go home. He's leaning on the rake, and you can tell he's paying attention, not like some grown-ups, like that girl in the mini-market last week, when you went there to buy milk for Mommy. You stood at the counter for, like, *hours*, and she just kept talking on her cell and laughing.

"*Twenty-five* Carbon Street," you say. "That's my house."

He nods. You don't want to be rude and stare at him while he's thinking, so you look around and check out his house. It's tall and narrow, with just one little window in front and another, even smaller window up on the second floor, and it's really old. It's all gray and weathery. The other house down the street looks like it's maybe even older. It's sagging into the ground, and all the windows are boarded up.

"Carbon Street is right near Hill Street," you say to kind of remind him that you're still waiting. "Do you know where that is?"

He shakes his head finally and says, "No, sorry."

"Oh," you say, disappointed. "Well, thank you, anyway."

You start walking back. It's a long block, but you're pretty sure that almost right after you turn the corner, there're lots more houses. You'll find somebody who'll know how to direct you to Carbon Street. Maybe some nice lady will even drive you there. Then you hear the man calling you, and you turn around, and say, "What?" And it's funny, because he didn't seem to recognize you, but you think you heard him say your name.

"I have a—" He stops, and you wait, and then he says, "I have a city map in the house."

"Oh," you say. "You do? That's great!" You walk back to him and say, "Can I see that map, please? I know how to read maps."

The man leans the rake against the porch. "Come on in, and we'll check it together."

You're pretty sure you shouldn't go in his house, and you start to say you'll wait outside. But he looks at you, frowning a little, and says, "Come on, then," in that voice that grown-ups have, not being mean, but when they get a little bit impatient with you.

So you hesitate just for a moment, and then you say, "Okay," because you don't want him to think you're scared or anything, and you go up the steps after him and follow him into his house.

PART
TWO
IN THE SHADOW
OF AUTUMN

SUNDAY AFTERNOON: ROOM
WITH A VIEW

THE MAN WATCHES his pretty one trying to open the door, rattling the doorknob. "Open the door, please," she says. "Please open the door. It's locked."

"Are you hungry?" he asks. He wants to feed her, take care of her.

She turns the doorknob again and again. "I want to go home now, please."

"No," he says quietly. "Not yet. You're going to be my guest."

"What?" she says. "Your what?"

"Guest," he repeats. "I have a room ready for you." He points upstairs. "The guest room. It's all ready."

"What?" she says again, and then she starts screaming. "Let me go," she screams. "Unlock the door, let me go, please let me *go*," she shrieks.

"Shh, shh," he says, moving toward her. "Please," he says. "Not so much noise."

Her face is bunched up, her mouth gaping. He's always been sensitive to noise, and his heart pumps too hard with every shriek. "Stop that noise," he says, but she just goes on screaming.

The cat Harold leaps up onto the table and arches his back. "Off," the man says. For a moment he's torn between the two badly behaving creatures. He brushes the cat off the table with the side of his arm and reaches for his girl. "Stop that now, that's enough," he says, and he takes her by the arms. She wriggles and screeches and screams.

When she won't stop, he's forced to slap her. He doesn't want to do it, but she pushed him to it. Still, he's not out of control. He didn't hit her too hard, and when she stumbles and falls, he leaves her on the floor for only a minute or two, to learn her lesson. Then he reaches down and helps her up. Her nose is bleeding. She's crying, blubbering, which is almost as unpleasant as her screams. She's leaking all over her face. Snot, blood, tears, spit. It's disgusting.

"Here," he says, and thrusts his handkerchief at her. "Wipe yourself."

She blots her eyes and says something: "Please let me go," or "Can I go home now?" Something like that, but he isn't really listening. He's just noticed her fingernails, which are long and painted a repulsive pink. He'll have to cut them, but that's for later.

"We're going upstairs now," he says, taking her by the hand.

"No," she says, dragging her feet. "No, I don't want to, I don't want to."

She's forcing him again to do something he had no intention of doing. He pulls her into the kitchen, where he finds a piece of rope in the back of a drawer and, with some effort, because she refuses to cooperate, he ties her wrists together. "Behave," he says quietly.

"Let me go!" she screams. "Let me go!"

"I don't want to do this," he says, slapping her. She continues screaming. He has to slap her again. And again, harder. A few more slaps and she quiets down. After that everything is better.

He leads her up the stairs by the rope, and she follows quietly. This is the way he wants it—comfortable, nice, both of them getting along.

"You're the first guest," he says, opening the door and pulling her into the room. "Do you like it?" She doesn't answer. "It's clean," he assures her. He closes the door behind them. "Look at that window," he says. "This is a room with a view."

The small, uncurtained window looks out over the back of the property. Some brushy stuff, the ravine, trees, the mountains. It can be quite beautiful. He could probably rent this room without any trouble. Of course, he'd have to get a few things, a chest of drawers, maybe a mirror and a rug. Right now there's only a canvas army cot standing against one wall and the bucket. That's all she's going to need. But even if she wasn't here, he wouldn't rent. Not a good idea. All he'd need to turn his life upside down was one snoop, one eager citizen who fancied himself an investigator.

He points to the bucket. "That's the facility. Put on the cover after you use it."

She nods. Her eyes are big. Big and beautiful and wet.

"Don't cry," he says. "I don't like crying."

She whispers, "I won't."

"Good girl." He strokes her hair. She shivers.

"Don't be afraid," he says. "You don't have to be afraid of me." She nods and shivers and blinks her big wet eyes.

SUNDAY AFTERNOON: CAN ANYBODY HEAR ME?

THE MAN UNTIES your wrists. You shake your hands to get the blood going again, and it feels so good to have the rope off that you blurt, "Thank you."

"You're a good girl," he says, and he tells you that you're a polite girl and he likes polite girls. He says it like he's your father or something. Only Poppy never hit you. Poppy never, ever, in his life did anything mean to you.

After the man takes off the rope, he leaves. He locks you in, and you're so glad he's gone you almost pee in your pants. You use the bucket, and it's gross, and you're afraid he can hear the pee hitting the sides.

You pull up your jeans and look around. You see faded

wallpaper with big white sailing ships, you see a cot, and that's it. There's nothing else in this room to even look at, except the pail you just peed in. The cot is one of those sorry old army cots, rough brown canvas and heavy wood, like the one Poppy has in the garage for when he's working on his pickup truck and wants to take a rest.

"Poppy," you whisper, and then your eyes fasten on the single, small window, and you stand on tiptoes to look out, and what you see makes you want to cry. What you see is *nothing*. Just bushes and trees. Trees, trees, trees. No streets. No sidewalks. No houses. *No people.*

Just below the window is a slanted metal roof, and you squint your eyes and imagine yourself sliding down the roof, right down to the ground. You push at the window, trying to open it, but you can't budge it. Either the window's too high, or you're too short, or you're not strong enough, or all of the above. Maybe you could open it if you could get up on the sill, but you know you can't do that, either. It's like how you can't climb the ropes in phys ed. The first time, you knew it before you even tried.

If only you could yell for Poppy. If he heard you, he'd come and get you so fast that man wouldn't have a chance to even *squeak*! There's no way Poppy can hear you, but you yell, anyway. "Help! Help me!" you scream, and you pound on the window. "Help, help! Can anybody hear me?"

"I hear you," the man says, closing the door behind him.

You shrink away into a corner.

"Keeping yourself busy?" he says in a normal, regular voice, like he's your friend.

You crouch down, making yourself small, and bundle your arms around your legs. He smiles at you, like you're doing something cute, and he locks the door and puts the key in his pocket.

Now you see that he's carrying a hammer. He takes a nail out of his pocket and hammers it into the window frame. He takes another nail out of his pocket and hammers it in above the first nail. More nails. More hammering. You don't get it. Then you do.

He's nailing the window shut. He's nailing you in.

SUNDAY AFTERNOON: GOOD AND LOUD

ALL DAY BEAUTY was caught in a cooking frenzy. In a way it started with Autumn's missing out on the pancakes. Around noon, after everyone had finished eating, Beauty made another batch of batter and put it away in the refrigerator for Autumn. Poor kid, by the time she came home, she'd be starved. Then, thinking about the sister she was really feeling sorry for, Beauty turned on the oven and assembled the makings for chocolate chip cookies. Flour, sugar, butter, baking powder, chocolate chips.

When Mim came downstairs to refill her water bottle, Beauty was spooning little mounds of dough, lumpy with chocolate chips, onto the cookie trays. Mim wiped her finger around the rim of the batter bowl, licked, and went for one of the doughy lumps. Beauty slapped her hand away. "No! They're for Stevie."

"Make some for us, too," Mim urged. "Comfort food. We all need it, big-time."

Beauty made more dough, enough to fill another two cookie trays. Once the cookies were baked, she could have left the kitchen, maybe should have, but she opened the cookbook and decided to make corn bread to go with the fricassee she was planning for supper.

She was aware of what she was doing—keeping herself busy so she wouldn't brood over Stevie's leaving and the hole it would make in their family. Weren't they all dealing with the Stevie thing in their own ways? If hers was cooking, Autumn's was not showing up for a meal. Mim had buried herself in her books all day, their father had disappeared into the garage, and for hours their mother had been unraveling a knitted blanket. As for Beauty's *object of desire,* even he had retreated, sacking out on the couch. Only Fancy seemed fairly unaffected. Sure, she'd cried the night Beauty had broken the news about Stevie, but did she really get it? Probably not.

Around three thirty, when Autumn still hadn't come home, her mother was fretting, which meant chain-smoking, which Beauty hated. "Mom, don't worry," she said. "Autumn's probably right down the block somewhere or with her girlfriends."

"She's going to hear from me when she gets home," her mother said. "She needs a good smacking."

"Mom, calm down," Beauty said. Then she sent Fancy outside to call Autumn. "Just stand out there and yell for her, honey," Beauty said. "Good and loud." That had worked plenty of times in the past.

SUNDAY EVENING: FINGERS AND TOES

THE MAN SAYS, "Sit down." He points to the cot. He's still holding the hammer.

You unfold yourself from the corner and creep across the room. You keep your eyes on him. He stands there by the window, his arm on the sill, and watches you.

You sit down on the edge of the cot, which gives a little under your weight. You try not to blink or cry or shake or anything, but your fingers are tapping on your leg. *Tap, tap, tap*. You can't stop them. You can't keep them still.

"Are you comfortable?" he says.

What does he mean? At first you thought that he was taking you for a hostage, like on TV. You wanted to tell him your family isn't rich, but you were too scared to say anything. And now . . . well, now you don't think it's about money.

"Are you comfortable?" he says again.

"I guess so," you whisper.

He gets down on his knees in front of you. He puts his hands on your hands and makes them stop tapping. He stares at you. You say, "Please don't hurt me."

"Don't be a stupid girl," he says. He unties your sneakers. He takes them off and peels off your socks. Your socks are stinky, and for a moment you wish that you'd put on a clean pair this morning.

"Naughty girl," he says in his quiet voice. "Dirty feet." His voice is always the same. He doesn't sound mad or disgusted, but then he smacks the bottoms of your feet, first one, then the other. You cry out. "Shh," he admonishes.

He picks up your feet and rubs them on his cheeks. Then he kisses your dirty feet, first one, then the other, and he says, "That's how much I love you."

SUNDAY EVENING: SURE
AND POSITIVE AND POSITIVE
AND SURE

WHEN BEAUTY CAME back from her walk around the neighborhood, looking for Autumn, the fricassee she'd made for supper was just about done. She poked her head into her sisters' bedroom. It was past five and getting dark outside. "Did Autumn say anything to either of you about where she was going?"

"Not *meee*," Fancy sang out. She stabbed a needle into a button she was sewing on one of her stuffed animals.

Stevie, who was on her knees repacking her duffle again—she'd been at it all day, adding and subtracting items—shook her head.

"You okay?" Beauty asked, kneeling down next to her.

"Sure," Stevie said, giving her a bitter look. Her eyes were all swollen. "I'm just great."

"I'm so sorry, honey," Beauty said, not for the first time.

Stevie looked at her for a moment, then turned away.

Beauty stood up. *She* should be the one going to live with Aunt Bernie. *She* adjusted to change, to disruption, to everything, more easily than Stevie. For a moment it seemed completely doable. Throw some things into a suitcase, get her records from school, tell the family she was taking Stevie's place, and—

But no, it wasn't that simple. She brought money into the household that the family needed, and what about the way her mother depended on her to watch out for her sisters and to take care of another thousand things. Besides, was she really ready to throw away her graduation, just like that? To be utterly honest, no. Selfishly, *no*. She had worked for it, she had waited for it too long to sacrifice, even for Stevie.

"Fancy, come and set the table," she said, more sharply than she meant to speak. She steered Fancy into the kitchen. "Are you sure Autumn didn't say anything to you about where she was going?" she asked.

"I'm sure."

"Positive? Think hard."

"I'm positive and sure and sure and positive," Fancy chanted.

"Okay, fine." Beauty tasted the fricassee and added salt, reminding herself again that this wasn't the first time that Autumn would be late for a meal. Usually it was no big deal, although her mother always fretted, but tonight was different. It would be Stevie's last meal with the family for months. At least they could all be there for her.

SUNDAY EVENING: SUPPER'S SERVED

THE MAN BRINGS you food. The food is on a paper plate, which he sets down on the floor on newspapers. "Your tablecloth," he says. He's making a joke. "Go ahead, eat," he says. "Supper's served. "

You look at the newspapers on the floor. You look at the food. Crackers, a hunk of cheese with blue stuff in it, and a wrinkled tomato. How do you know the food isn't poisoned? For maybe the first time in your life, you have no appetite.

"Are you going to eat?" the man asks.

You shake your head.

He frowns and pulls at his tie. "I'll leave it for now," he

says, and he opens the door. You catch a glimpse of a cat. "I'm going to have my supper now," he says, as if it's something you really want to know. He goes out. He locks the door.

You've never been locked in anywhere. You walk from the door to the window, from the window to the door. It's like you're a prisoner. No, you *are* a prisoner. You're in jail, and you haven't even done anything wrong.

You walk around the room, around and around. It's like being in a cage, like you're a hamster. But if you're a hamster, your brain is a monkey, and it's going around and around, too. It's your monkey brain that says, *Maybe this is just another story you're making up and you're inside it.* You want to believe it. But if this is a story, why does your face still smart from his slaps? Why do your wrists still burn like real life? And if this is a story, when do you get the happy ending?

SUNDAY EVENING: SUPPER'S SERVED

FANCY MADE A BIG thing out of setting the table, putting the silverware just so, folding the napkins like birds and sticking them in the water glasses, but it was finally done. Mim had emerged from her story stupor, and she made herself useful putting out the bread and butter and finding the grated cheese container, which had been misplaced way in the back of the lowest shelf in the refrigerator. She'd also rounded everyone up, going through the house calling, "Supper. Supper, supper's served."

Now they were all present at the table except Autumn. "Where is that girl?" Blossom fretted. "She knows it's supper time."

"She has no business staying out so late," Beauty's father added. He'd showered, and his hair was wet and slicked down. "She's done this before," he said, frowning at Blossom. "You have to have a talk with her. You let her get away with too much."

Beauty's mother flushed and said quickly, "I've told her a thousand times she's supposed to be at the table with everyone else. Sometimes she just doesn't listen."

"Dad, you know how she is." Beauty automatically sprang to Autumn's defense. "She just gets into a dream and forgets everything. She doesn't mean to be late."

"But she is. I'm going to go look for her," her father said, pushing away from the table, and he went out.

While that conversation was going on, Nathan had been telling Stevie that he wanted to make an early start the next morning. "Okay with you?" he asked. She shrugged. "Still not talking to me?" he said. "It's going to be a long silent trip, darlin'."

"Good," Stevie muttered.

Beauty had put the fricassee on the table in a large bowl with her mother's best serving spoon, one of the few really nice things they had. It was silver and had been her grandmother's. She wanted this meal, Stevie's last with the family for a long time, to be special. After her father left the table, she was uncertain if they should start eating without him and Autumn, but her mother nodded at her to pass around the bowl. She gave it to Stevie first, who took a single chicken wing and passed the bowl right on to Fancy.

"I looove fricassee," Fancy said, and started picking out meatballs and ignoring the chicken wings.

Beauty looked across the table at Nathan. Had she really said all that stupid stuff about him to Mim? She was such a leaf in the wind when it came to men! At least she hadn't told Mim *who* was the object of her desire.

When the bowl had gone around the table, she covered it with a plate to keep the food warm. Silverware clinked. Stevie got up and went to the sink for a glass of water. Nathan was talking to Blossom.

Listening for the sound of her father returning with Autumn, Beauty checked the time again. Autumn would be in tears, for sure, sorry for upsetting her Poppy, sorry for upsetting everyone, but sorriest of all for herself. Beauty decided that, for once, Autumn's tears were not going to soften her into sympathy. She should be here for this meal. Period. No excuses. Sure, she was upset about

Stevie, but so were they all. No, no sympathy this time. It was bratty of Autumn to stay out this long, to worry her parents, to draw attention to herself, just plain bratty, and unfair to Stevie.

SUNDAY EVENING, LATER:
WASTE NOT, WANT NOT

YOU'RE SITTING ON the cot when the man comes back. You've put your sneakers back on. You tied them tight. Your feet are flat on the floor.

He looks at the food you didn't eat. He clicks his tongue and wraps the food in the newspaper. "Waste not, want not," he says. "You'll eat tomorrow morning."

You don't say anything, but you hate the way that he says "tomorrow morning."

Then he says it again. "You'll eat tomorrow morning."

Now you understand that he's asking a question, that he wants an answer, that he wants you to say you'll eat. You don't want to talk, so you nod.

"Good girl," he says, as if you're a dog that just learned a new trick. "Lie down now and go to sleep."

You shake your head. You don't want to lie down. You don't want to move. You just want to sit there with your feet flat on the floor, and your arms crossed over your belly.

"Lie down," he says again.

Your stomach flutters. "I'm . . . not sleepy," you say.

He gives your shoulders a little shove, and then another. He takes off your sneakers. He took away your stinky socks before. He kisses your feet. He strokes your hair, then your face. You lie there, waiting for him to stop.

When he leaves, he locks you in again.

You listen to his footsteps going away. You can hear him going down the stairs. You slip off the cot and pick up your sneakers, and you sit down on the floor, holding them. Not putting them on, just holding them. He told you not to cry, but tears keep leaking out of your eyes. And you're glad, because those tears belong to you. They're *yours*. Your tears. He can't have them. He can't touch them. They're all yours.

SUNDAY NIGHT, LATE: IT WAS JUST A WALK

IT'S DARK AND quiet. You slept for a while, but now you're awake, and for a moment you don't know where you are or why it's so dark. Then you remember, and your stomach squeezes up into your throat. You stumble off the cot and half crawl to the bucket, but it smells of your pee, and you don't even want to throw up in it. You sit on the floor, weeping for a long time, and then you crawl back onto the cot and huddle under the hateful-smelling blankets and try to understand why you're locked in this room and not home in your own bed.

Okay, you were mad, you admit it, mad at them all, and you took a walk, but that's it. *It was just a walk*. You didn't do anything wrong. Okay, you should have told Mommy you were going out, you can see that now. You put your hands together under your chin and whisper to God, "If You get me out of this, I promise I'll never do that again."

You wait for an answer, as if God doesn't have a million other things to do besides worrying about you. Does God know how everything changed so fast? Does God know about the man? You hope so.

Tears sting your cheeks where he hit you. You close your eyes. You want to sleep. You want to sleep so you can forget the man and where you are and how, when you wake up tomorrow morning, you'll still be here.

MONDAY MORNING:
FEET FIRST

IN THE MORNING he stands in the doorway and beckons you to come to him.

"What?" you say. You hold on to the cot with both hands.

He crooks his finger. "Come on. Come on over here. Taking a little trip."

Your stomach thuds. "Where are we going?"

"Come on. You'll see, nosy girl." His voice is still nice. "Just come on now."

You walk toward him. Your legs are shaky. He motions for you to go in front of him. He puts his hands on your shoulders, steers you down the steep, narrow staircase. At the bottom of the stairs, you remember, is a little hall and then the front door.

The front door. You remember walking through it, following him into this house. It's that door that stands between you and home. Is he going to open the door? Is he taking you down there to let you go? He's says he's a nice man. Maybe, right now, he's going to prove it to you.

He squeezes your shoulders, and it hurts a little, but you don't care because *he's going to let you go*. You're sure of it. Why else would he be taking you down these stairs? You're almost there now. When he opens the door, you'll walk through it, onto the porch, down the steps, out to the sidewalk. And then you'll run.

Wait.

If he thinks that you'll tell on him, that could make him change his mind and not let you go. Okay, you'll just say to him that you won't tell. *Nobody. On my honor. I promise, no matter what they ask me. I'll just say I stayed with a nice man for a while when I got lost, okay? Is that good?*

While you're thinking this, he steers you past the front door and through his living room.

"Wait," you say. "I won't tell."

He keeps pushing you along through the room, past a

chair and a TV. A cat is sleeping on the floor near the chair. "That's Harold," he says, and he pushes you into a bathroom.

"Wash yourself," he says. He points to the sink. "Hands, face, feet. Feet first."

He hands you a cloth and watches you wash your feet. He watches you wash your hands and face. For a moment, bending over the basin and splashing water on your face, you pretend you're home, and any moment your sisters will bang on the door and yell at you to hurry up, you aren't the only one who needs the bathroom.

"All right, darling, enough," he says, and he hands you a towel. He tells you to hang the towel on the towel bar. He marches you back up the stairs, back to the room. He locks you in.

MONDAY AFTERNOON:
ANSWER ME

YOU HEAR SCRATCHING at the door. You lie down on the floor and stick your fingers under the door. "Cat, hello," you say. "Hello, cat." You wriggle your fingers. "Are you out there?" You wait, your throat tight. "Cat, cat," you call, "answer me, cat. Answer me, please!" Your voice rises. "Are you there? Why don't you answer me?"

You slump over on your arms. You hate that cat. It's his. You hate everything that's his. You hate this room. You hate the cot. You hate the blanket. You hate the pail and the walls and the floor and the window. You hate it all, hate it, hate it.

You lie there, stretched out. You don't move. You weigh a thousand pounds. You can never move again. You lie there. You listen to yourself breathing. You listen to the silence of the house. Your eyes are wet and burning.

MONDAY AFTERNOON:
EVERYTHING IS CRAZY

HELLO! I'M HAVING The Urge because everything is crazy and mixed up. *One!* No New Hampshire
because Stevie my sister screamed at everybody like this,
I'M NOT GOING ANYWHERE TODAY, YOU CAN'T
MAKE ME. *Two!* Cousin Nathan says he will stay, too.
Three! Mommy gave Stevie my sister a slap for screaming
and a hug for staying. *Four!* Poppy says, Don't worry,
Fancy baby, Autumn'll be back soon. *Five!* They think I
don't know anything like what *disappear* means.

Ha-ha! I know what it means. It means gone, good-bye,
invisible, which is a big word, which I can rhyme funny,
like invisible, delisible, halisible. I know how to do rhyme

stuff, because *I am not* dumb. I can read. I can read Nancy Drew. I can read Frog and Toad. I can read the funnies. Mrs. Sokolow my teacher says, "Good for you, Fancy, you're working hard at your reading. I'm proud of you."

But today she can't say, "Good for you, Fancy," because everybody stays home from school, and that makes me mad as boiling hornets. My family is *sooo* stupid. Stupid all of them. Stupid Autumn! Why does she disappear? Beauty my sister wiped my mouth that was all spitty, and she said, "Come on, Fancy, cool off. Don't give me that look, okay? We're all staying home today. Just be good and don't get people upset."

Right! Best day of the week, Monday, and no school. Right! Mommy doesn't go to work. Right! Nathan my cousin doesn't go away to New Hampshire with Stevie my sister. Right! And the telephone is ringing and never stopping. Everything is crazy.

MONDAY EVENING: 'FESS UP

THE DOOR OPENS. "Hello," he says. He's carrying a chair.

You're sitting on the cot. Your feet are on the floor. Your hands are biting into each other.

He puts down the chair. "Did you miss me?" he asks. "Did you miss me today?" He puts his hands on his hips, and he smiles his half smile at you. "Come on, Autumn, 'fess up."

Slowly you shake your head.

"Oh, oh, oh," he says, playfully. "You're teasing me. I know you missed me. Alone here all day? You missed me." He sits down on the chair and pats his legs. "Come here," he says. "Come over here and sit with Daddy. *Come on,*" he says.

Your heart is going *booom booom booom booom.* You're going to have a heart attack. You're going to die. Will your family ever know what happened to you? You remember all the times you played Dead Person, so you could make up the story of how your sisters and parents would cry and say how much they loved you and how sorry they were for not being nicer to you.

"Right here," he says.

You sit on his lap.

He takes off your sneakers. He kisses your feet.

MONDAY EVENING: IN NATHAN'S TRUCK

BEAUTY SAT WITH her face pressed to the side window as Nathan slowly steered his pickup truck past the old opera house and over the North Branch bridge.

"What time is it?" her father asked. He was sitting between them.

"Seven thirty, Dad," Beauty said.

He nodded. They had been driving around Mallory for over an hour. Futile, really. Did they think they'd just come across Autumn strolling down some side street, or waiting for them in front of their school? But they had to do something. It was too awful to go on sitting at home, looking at one another, all of them thinking their own separate, terrible thoughts.

Beauty sat forward, peering into the darkness, willing herself to believe that nothing awful had happened to her sister, that the child had run away. Which was bad, but not horrendous. After all, how far could she get on foot? That little chub was not an athlete.

Say she slept in a field last night. Say she realized how silly she'd been. Say they'd find her tonight, maybe on Route 11, walking back toward Mallory, tired, but glad to be found. Say all that, and try to believe it.

TIMES STAR

Established 1899

"I may not agree with what you say, but I'll defend to the death your right to say it."

POLICE SEEK INFORMATION ON MISSING MALLORY GIRL

Mallory—Police are looking for information that would lead to the whereabouts of a Carbon Street child who was reported missing late Sunday evening. Autumn Herbert, 11, was last seen Sunday morning, when she left her home at approximately 11 A.M., according to Detective Kurt Brantley of the Mallory Police Department. Detective Brantley said the 5th-grade girl was reported missing by her distraught mother. So far police have been unable to locate anyone who has seen her since she left her home on Carbon Street.

Detective Brantley described the girl as 5'2", weighing 135 pounds, with waist-length brown hair and hazel eyes. She was last seen wearing blue jeans with embroidered flowers on the back pockets, a yellow T-shirt, a red jacket, and white sneakers with a red blaze on the heel, Brantley said.

Anyone with information is asked to contact Detective Brantley at the Mallory Police Department (555-3166) or call Crime Stoppers (555-3513).

TUESDAY MORNING: SLEEPING
AND CRYING AND SINGING

HE'S GONE, AND you've been sleeping. You had a dream about Poppy and Fancy, and they were talking to you, and you were happy. And then you woke up.

All morning, when you're not sleeping, you're crying. You think S&C. When you're not S&C, you peel strips of wallpaper. You peel carefully, trying to peel off whole sections with the sailing ship that reminds you of that song Poppy sings, the one that always makes you smile and tear up at the same time.

"'Four strong winds that blow lonely,'" you sing, "'seven seas that run high.'" Your voice wobbles, but you go on. "'All these things that won't change, come what may. Well, our good times are all gone—'" You never really thought about those lines before, but now the words make a jagged lump in your stomach, and you go back to peeling wallpaper, and keep T&F—trying and failing—to get yourself up on the windowsill.

You curl up on the cot, and you're crying again. You hold yourself, and you cry and cry, and your eyes ache, and your face is all tight and swollen. And you remember how Poppy always told you, *Crying don't do you one bit of good and plenty of not good.*

Then and there, you make up your mind. You're not going to cry again.

Later, you find yourself wishing he'd bring you an apple.

Wishing he'd let you watch TV.

Wishing he'd take you outside, even for five minutes.

And you find yourself thinking how you'll ask him for these favors in your nicest voice, and how he'll say *yes, yes,* and *yes.*

TUESDAY EVENING:
MY ADVENTURE

HELLO! HERE I am with The Urge, because I had an adventure, and when Autumn my sister isn't disappeared anymore, I'll tell my adventure to Mrs. Sokolow my teacher, and she'll say, "Fancy, good for you! Stand up here in front of the class and tell everyone your adventure."

And I will! I'll tell everybody I was in a car with two police, and we drove around different streets, and the man police said, "Honey, keep looking out the window, okay? And tell us if you see anybody that talked or acted funny with you and your sister."

And then the lady police asked me a bazillion questions, like, "Where did you go with your sister? What places? What did you two do? Did anybody talk to you?"

I told her lots of people talk to us, and sometimes we go to the candy store, and sometimes we go to the park, and I feed the cute little baby ducks with bread that the nice man gives me, and baby ducks are *sooo* cute.

I was just saying nice things, but the lady police said the F-swear, and the man police said, "Laura, please," and the lady police said, "Chris, we're not going to get anything worthwhile from her."

Which meant me, and she thought I didn't know, but I did, and when I go back to school again, I'm going to tell everyone about going in the police car, even Kevin Farley, who just shakes his head all day long and doesn't like me. And Mrs. Sokolow my teacher will say, "Good for you, Fancy. You had an adventure!"

TUESDAY EVENING: FIDDLEHEADS

HE NOTICES THE red bumps on your hands. He says, "What's that rash on your hands?" and you say it's probably from being under the blanket without a sheet.

He brings you a sheet. He wants you to say thank you. You say it.

He wants you to say he's a nice man. You say it.

You ask if you could have a pillow, too. He says he'll think about it. "If you're a good girl, maybe."

He puts you on his lap.

You go away, you float out of your body and swim along the ceiling and float right out the window, and you're with Poppy in his truck, taking a ride to find fiddleheads, which

Poppy likes to do every spring. Fiddleheads are like free vegetables, and you're the one who most likes to go with Poppy to find them down by the creek, where the ferns grow in the marshy places.

Mommy is always happy when you and Poppy bring back a bag of the funny coiled little green things. "They charge eight bucks a pound for them things at the market," she says, kissing Poppy on the cheek because he's so smart. And she cooks them with cabbage and carrots and makes a nice gravy, and you and your sisters and Mommy and Poppy all sit down and are so nice and happy together.

WEDNESDAY MORNING:
BORED LONELY

HE OPENS THE door and crooks his finger. You pick up the pail. He walks you down the stairs, his hands on your shoulders.

After he takes you back to the room, he brings you food. He spreads the newspapers and makes the tablecloth joke. He puts down a small box of cornflakes, a glass of water, and a banana. He doesn't like milk, and he won't buy it. He watches you eat the dry cornflakes. When you're done, he says, "Was it good?"

"Yes," you lie. You're still hungry. You'll be hungry all day.

"How about a smile?" he says.

You make a smile.

"Nice," he says. "You should always smile." He smoothes his tie. He's wearing pressed pants, a blue shirt with white stripes, a blue flowered tie, a black cardigan sweater. His face is all shaved and clean. His hair is combed neatly. If you didn't know, you'd think he was a teacher or a minister.

He pets your hair, then he looks at his watch, and he says, "You be a good girl while I'm gone." You don't say anything. "Are you going to be a good girl while I'm gone?" he asks. You say, "Yes."

He pets your hair again or maybe he doesn't, because he starts twisting your hair around his hand. He twists it and twists it, until you cry out, "You're hurting me."

Later, you're so bored, so lonely, you find yourself:
- looking forward to going downstairs
  (someplace other than this room)
- wondering about supper (maybe there'll
  be something different)
- thinking about his return.

Thinking about his return? And then it hits you. You're getting used to being a prisoner.

WEDNESDAY, MID-MORNING: FREAKS

SITTING ON THE floor in the living room, Beauty was staring blankly at a TV show in which two women were yelling at each other about the man sitting between them. It was a freak show, hair falling around the faces of the furious women, their hands clawing the air, while the man sat there, his arms folded, a little smile on his face.

This was the third day Autumn had been missing. The third day Beauty and her sisters had stayed home from school. Beauty had made the decision. "We can't go to school. We wouldn't be able to concentrate on anything." By now they had all stopped crying. They roamed the house, restless, or stared at the TV. They forgot meals, but neighbors brought them food, or they ate popcorn and chips. They were in waiting mode. Waiting for the police, waiting for someone, for *anyone* to bring them Autumn, or at least news of her. And silently Beauty prayed, *Good news, please. Make it good news.*

The phone rang, and Beauty leaped up, although it was probably just Jane Russo, the reporter from the Mallory paper, who called a few times every day to ask if they'd heard anything.

"What is it with you people?" a man said on the other end of the line. "What'd you do with her? You bunch of freaks, you shitty people, you child abusers, you better—"

Beauty slammed down the phone. She was shaking.

WEDNESDAY AFTERNOON: TOUGH GUY

THAT FIRST DAY, when he led you up the stairs like a dog on a leash? You thought he was taking you hostage. You were young then.

Was it Monday or Tuesday when you imagined yourself leaping into the air and karate kicking straight through the window? *Ka-booom!* You imagined yourself sailing out, landing on your toes, taking off for home. You were young then.

You ball up your fists and bang on the window. "Break, damn it," you scream. The window stares back at you with a blank face. Like his face, you think.

You trot around the room. You're a horse. Around you go. Once, twice, three times, six times, ten times.

You're a kickboxer. You kick the cot with each pass.

You're a tough guy. You run, smashing your hand against the wall. Your hand hurts, but you're a tough guy. You trot faster, wall to wall to wall, kicking, screaming, smashing.

WEDNESDAY EVENING: WHEN . . .

YOU HEAR HIM outside the door . . .

you see the door knob turning . . .

you watch the door opening . . .

your eyes swing around the room, corner to corner to corner, as if there's someplace to hide.

There isn't.

You don't move. Your hands bite into each other.

He's carrying the chair.

WEDNESDAY EVENING: WHAT DOES HE WANT?

THE MAN STANDS at the sink, washing dishes and listening to the sound of her little feet above his head. He's read about men who do bad things to little girls. He's not like them. He's just a lonely man. He's always been lonely, except for eight years ago when he also had a little girlfriend. He's tried to obliterate her and her red curly hair from his memory. It ended badly. That little girl wasn't nice. Because of her, he lost his freedom for five years. Five bad years. He pulls the plug on the sink, yanks it up hard.

He doesn't like to think about that, or what happened when he got out, either. How he was supposed to report in constantly. How no one wanted him to live near them. How they put signs on his car. How he couldn't get a job. A miserable, miserable time. It's all behind him now, *like a bad dream*. He came through it, though. Took himself away from that poisonous atmosphere, and now he has a new name, a home, a job, and, best of all, he's not lonely. Thanks to her! After all, it's her doing that she's here. He didn't do anything to make it happen. She came to him, walked right up to him, didn't she? As good as invited herself into his life.

He picks up a blue plastic mug. Hers. She's coming along, getting used to things, not like the first day when she would hardly speak, just kept crying, her face all snotty and wet. And the sounds she made! Cat sounds. Piercing, mewling cries that sent shivers into the palate of his mouth.

The cats regard him, one from under the table, one from the top of the refrigerator. Violet's a climber. The male is exactly the opposite, always under things. To each his own, the man thinks. Every cat, every man, wants something different. And what does *he* want? He holds the blue plastic mug to his lips. He wants her to be his. To sit on his lap. He wants to stroke her hair, her face, her arms and legs. He wants her to be happy that she's here. He holds the mug against his lips a moment longer, then places it carefully in the dish rack.

WEDNESDAY EVENING: BLOODY HELL

THE SPRAY OF THE headlights briefly lit up the ditches, the rutted road, the sprawl of trees. Beauty's eyes ached from peering into the thick darkness. Next to her Mim was a small, solid presence, leaning close, looking out the window with her. The truck hit a rock or maybe a dead animal and lurched to one side of the narrow road. "Bloody hell," Nathan said for at least the third time. "These roads are worse than New Hampshire."

"But this is a good old truck," Mim said, patting the seat. She was sitting between Beauty and Nathan. "What's its name?"

"Name?" Nathan said, as if the word were from a foreign language.

"You didn't name it?" Mim said. "When I get my pickup truck, I'm going to name it."

"Crazy," Nathan said, and laughed.

Beauty shifted. She knew Mim was trying to keep Nathan calm. Already, twice, he'd said they should give up this "crazy search" and go home. And now he said it again.

"It's getting late. How about we call it a night?"

"No!" Beauty said, and then more quietly, "Please. Not yet."

Four days had passed since Autumn disappeared. Vanished, as if she'd been swept up and off the face of the earth. Beauty had little hope that this needle-in-a-haystack search, this trawling from the truck and praying for *something*, would produce the miracle of finding her sister, but it was unbearable to stay in the house, hour after hour, day after day, night after night, and do nothing.

Nathan slowly steered the truck down the dark country road. They might have been anywhere—or nowhere. The road curved, went uphill, then down again. They approached a lit farmhouse, passed it and the looming shape of a barn, then darkness descended again. The road grew narrower still, ruts grabbed the tires, and suddenly Nathan pulled over to the shoulder and cut the engine.

"You know this is stupid, don't you?" he said. "Beauty. I'm talking to you. This is your idea, and I respect it, but it's stupid. I'm sorry, but it is. We have no idea where she is, or what we're doing on this road. She could be across the country for all we know, she could be—"

"Stop," Mim said. "Don't." Beauty felt her huddling closer.

"We're just wasting our time," he said quietly. He took off his cap and put it back on. "Come on, you girls know the cops are doing the real work. Am I right?"

Beauty didn't answer, just kept peering into the darkness. Was something moving there on the side of the road? She pressed her face harder against the cold window. Bushes. A few trees. Nothing else, not even an animal, but down the road, everything could change. It could happen. They could find her. Maybe stumbling along, lost. Maybe lying by the side of the road, left there . . . "Let's go," she said.

"Wait a second. Just tell me why we're here. I mean, why are we on this road?"

When Beauty was silent, Mim said, "It's something to do." She slid her hand into Beauty's. "It's something, isn't it, Beauty?"

"Yes," Beauty said. "It's something." That was it, exactly.

"Look," Nathan said, "I understand. You want to contribute, but like I said, we're just wasting time. Beauty, you listening? Why don't we just let the cops get on with it?"

At that moment headlights appeared in the distance. Slowly they grew stronger. Beauty stared, unblinking. Now she could hear the sound of the engine. For over an hour they hadn't seen a single car, yet here was this one, coming steadily on, straight toward them.

Beauty watched the hypnotically bright beams cutting the air, gripped by the thought that, at last, it was going to happen. Something momentous was about to take place. *That car was bearing Autumn toward her.* She threw open the door and leaped out of the truck. She ran down the middle of the road toward the car.

"What are you doing?" Nathan shouted. And she heard Mim, too. "Beauty, wait!"

She ran straight into the headlights, waving her arms. The car stopped, and a man looked out the window. "You need help?"

Beauty leaned on the hood, breathing hard, bracing herself with both hands. "My sister," she said. "I'm looking for my—"

"Say what?" The man had a bushy beard, wore a red-checked cap. "Are you stuck? I have a cell, I can call a tow truck."

"No, it's not that." He was alone. Or was he? She went around to the passenger side and peered into the car. A big dog slept on the backseat, his head on his paws. Newspapers were piled next to him. Bottles littered the floor.

Beauty stepped back onto the shoulder of the road and waved the man off, but he didn't go. "Who's in that truck you just came barreling out of?" he said suspiciously.

"It's okay. It's my cousin and my sister."

"That her coming?" Mim was making her way down the road. Beauty nodded. "You sure everything's okay?" he said.

"Yes. I'm sorry I made you stop."

He shrugged and slowly pulled past her. Then Mim was there and took her arm. "Come on, Beauty," she said. "Come on." She walked her back to the truck, waited till she was seated, then got in herself and slammed the door.

"I guess it's okay if we go home now?" Nathan said, but he didn't turn the key in the ignition.

Beauty covered her eyes with her hands and rocked.

Now they would go back to the house without Autumn. And they would all go to sleep, and another night would pass without her littlest sister at home. "No. No. *No.*"

Nathan put his arm around her. "Take it easy," he said.

Beauty pressed herself against him. "Oh, please. Oh, please, oh, please," she heard herself wailing. She wanted *so much.* She wanted love, she wanted him . . . or someone. She didn't know what she wanted . . . but oh, yes, she did. She did! She wanted Autumn safe home.

Mim's hands were on her shoulders. "Beauty," she said, "Beauty," and the sound of her voice brought Beauty back to herself. Abruptly she was sober and moving away from Nathan. "Sorry," she gasped. "I'm sorry."

"It's nothing," he said, "don't worry." He turned the key in the ignition.

THURSDAY MORNING: NOTES

BEFORE SHE WENT downstairs to make breakfast that morning, Beauty wrote in the journal she sporadically kept: *I acted like a total jerk with N. last night. I don't know what got into me. I grabbed onto him. I don't know how I'm going to face him this morning.*

Nathan had been writing a note, too. She found it propped up on the kitchen table next to the cereal box.

Cousins, sorry to leave this way, but I'll lose my job if I don't get back. Thought it best to get an early start. It's a long drive. Thanks for the hospitality. If you change your mind about sending Stevie (or anyone) to Aunt Bernie, let me know. Anyway, keep in touch. I'm praying for you. Nathan

So he was gone. Had she driven him away? She thought so, but she was relieved. Her nighttime confession to Mim about him seemed like part of a distant and absurd past.

THURSDAY AFTERNOON:
THE DUCK POND

WHEN ETHAN SHOWED up at the front door, Beauty stared as if she couldn't quite figure out who he was. "Hey," Ethan said, a half smile slipping on and off his face, as if he couldn't quite figure out, not who he was, but why he was there.

Friday was the last time she had seen him. And now it was Thursday. Six days had passed. Six days which might as well have been six weeks or six months or six years. It seemed to her that she was no longer the same girl who had been in Ethan's house and who had signaled him over his parents' heads. How intensely that silly girl had felt the deprivation of not sitting with him! How much of her life that girl had wasted in false sorrow and self-pity. And even last night that girl had acted the fool with her cousin.

"Hey," Ethan said again.

"Hey," Beauty said.

"I'm sorry about your sister," he said. "I read in the newspaper—"

"Yes," she said.

"Is there anything I can—"

"No."

"Do you know anyth—"

"No. Nothing."

"No c-c-clues to—"

"No."

"Sorry," he said again. He touched her arm. "Want to go for a walk?"

She thought for a moment, then nodded. "Wait." She went back into the house to tell her mother.

"Walking? Who with?" her mother said. She had the ironing board set up in the kitchen.

"A friend from school."

"What's her name?"

"His name, Mom. Ethan Boswell. Remember I was at his house?"

Her mother put down the iron. "When will you be back?"

"I don't know—maybe an hour and a half." She ran her fingers over her mother's forehead, smoothing out the wrinkles. "Mom, it's perfectly safe." She handed her a rolled-up blouse from the basket. "I was thinking, we have to start living normally, even if—"

"I can't," her mother gasped.

Beauty nodded. "I know, but we have to at least try, don't we?"

Her mother's eyes filled. She unrolled the shirt on the board and picked up the iron. Then, after a moment, she said, "Go ahead. Go with your friend."

Friend? Walking toward the park with Ethan, Beauty questioned herself. Why had she agreed to this? She had nothing to say to Ethan, and he seemed to have nothing to say to her.

In the park, though, sitting across from each other on the seesaw, he had plenty to say. "My mother had a h-h-heart attack last year," he blurted. "It was terrible. You don't think your mother's going to land in the h-h-hospital, almost dying."

"No, I guess not," Beauty said. Why was he telling her this?

"People kept saying to me not to worry, she was strong, stuff like that. Then they would just go off and talk about other things."

Like you're doing, she thought, but didn't say.

"It seems like nobody really understands when something bad happens, unless it's happened to them. I mean, maybe they're sorry, but it's not them, it's not their mother."

"Or their sister," Beauty said tersely.

"Yeah, that's exactly what I mean. Take me, I'm real sorry about your sister, it's an awful thing, but you're living with it. I'll just go home and do my regular stuff. I know how that sounds, callous, but I don't mean it that way. I'm just trying to be h-h-honest," he said.

Beauty's perch on the seesaw was up. She stared down at Ethan. He sounded so pleased with himself, letting her know he was smart enough to understand that Autumn's disappearance didn't really affect him, though he was (of course) sorry about it. Her breath came fast. She wanted to scream. "Let me down," she said.

"You okay?" he said, lifting his legs and going up.

"No!" She hopped off.

The seesaw bounced Ethan down. "Ouchers," he said.

She didn't smile. "I'm going home." She walked away, fast.

He called her name, but she kept walking, didn't wave, didn't look back.

Later she knew her anger wasn't really at Ethan. It was at this limbo they were caught in, how helpless they were to do anything, to make anything happen, to change anything. Where was Autumn? Where? Where? *Where?* Later still she knew his honesty was a gift, which she wasn't ready to accept.

THURSDAY, LATE AFTERNOON:
THE COT

YOU'RE LYING ON the floor, under the cot. Hiding? Not now, he's not here now. Lying low? Sort of. You stare up at the canvas and pretty soon you're back home, and you're in the garage hanging out with Poppy. He's stretched out on his army cot, being restful, his hands linked behind his head. You're sitting on the stool, near him, telling him about your problems with spelling. Poppy says you don't get that from him, that he was a whiz speller in school. "Whiz speller," you say. "Wow."

Your voice breaks the spell. You're not in the garage anymore. You're under the cot that's *his*, in the locked room that's *his*, in the house that's *his*. Yesterday he told you his name. Wayne. Then he told you his secret name. Nelson. He said, "Now it's a secret between us. You and me." He said that you were the only person, *the only one*, who could call him Nelson. "If you want to," he said. "But maybe you like the name Wayne better?"

You said no, you didn't like the name Wayne better, because you knew that was what he wanted you to say, so you don't call him Wayne, but you don't call him Nelson, either. You don't call him anything.

You roll out from under the cot and suddenly you're shoving it around the room, scraping the wooden legs on the floor, shoving it and kicking at it, and then picking it up and dropping it. You didn't even know you could pick it up, that you were strong enough. You do it again, pick it up and drop it, and then you try to throw it, but you can't, it's way too bulky and awkward.

You clench your fists and spin around and scream and scream. You want to throw something. You *have* to throw something. You grab your sneakers and throw them at the wall and then you throw them at the window.

And that's when you get the idea.

PART
THREE
FLYING

FRIDAY, 7:30 A.M.

"BE GOOD," HE says. "I'm going to work now."

"Okay," you say. It's raining outside again. You hear it on the tin roof. He's still standing in the doorway, waiting for something else from you. You probably didn't say enough.

"I'll be good," you say. You say it meekly, the way he likes.

He nods, but he still doesn't leave. What's he waiting for now? You know. A smile. You produce a smile. He doesn't know it's fake, fake, *fake*. Mommy always knows, and she says that funny old-fashioned thing: "You're giving me the phony baloney." But it's better not to think about Mommy or anybody.

"Eat all your food," he says.

You nod. He waits. You say, "I will. I'll eat it all." You want him to leave. You give him another big fake smile.

"Do you want anything else?" He twirls his key chain, and you're almost hypnotized. The key to this room is on that chain. "Well?" he says.

You pull your eyes away from the key chain and give him the same answer as you did yesterday and the day before yesterday. "Could I watch TV? Could you bring the TV in here?"

"I told you—no TV." He uses the Dad Voice. "It's a bad influence. I meant—" He pauses to make sure you're listening. "—do you want anything else to eat?"

Despite his turndown on the TV, he likes it when you ask for something, so you say, "Cookies?" You know he's going to ask you what kind, so you say perkily, "Chocolate chip cookies are my favorite."

He makes an approving murmur, as if you just said something clever. He's happy. You can tell from the way his eyes change, and he has that little half smile on his face. "I'll bring you chocolate chip cookies tonight," he says. Now he has the Cozy Voice, the Just-You-and-Me Voice. "I'll bring them home and we'll share them."

You hate the way he says "share" and "home," but you know it's a good thing. It means he's not suspicious. He looks at his watch, then beckons you over to him. Your stomach clenches. You walk over slowly. "What?" you say, but you know.

He bends and kisses you on the mouth. "Good-bye," he says. "Be good."

"Yes," you say, and you give him one more fake smile. *The last one,* you think.

FRIDAY, 8:15 A.M.

YOU KNOW that he left. You know that he's not in the house, but you stand near the door and listen. What if he guessed what you're going to do and sneaked back in to catch you at it? You hear creaks and thumps. Your heart thumps, too.

You put your mouth against the door and yell, "Hello? Hello?" If he's in the house, he'll hear you, and he'll come to see what you want. "Hello! Hello! Hello!"

You listen. Nothing. You're alone. Your stomach is ticking like a clock.

You throw the blanket off the cot and go to work on freeing the wooden bar at the end. The bar is joined to the wooden side pieces, and it resists you. You push and tug and pull, and after a while your hands are raw, your eyes sting from sweat, and you just want to sit down and cry. You do the sitting down part, but you don't do the crying part. You look out the rain-splattered window at the dark sky. Is it better for you that it's raining?

You get up and go back to the cot and try again. You get one hand on the bar and one hand on the side piece. You take a huge breath and pull with all your might, and the bar comes free. You take the wooden bar in both your sweaty hands like a baseball bat and smash it into the wall, and that feels *great*. You go into a frenzy of smashing. This wall. That wall. All the walls. Time is passing. You shouldn't be doing this. It's the window you want to break, not the walls. *The window.* You stop yourself, panting, and wipe the sweat from your eyes.

You raise the bat over your head and swing. Not hard enough. You raise it again, scream, and swing. And the window explodes. Glass is everywhere, splinters of glass on the floor and in your hair and stuck in your skin. Tiny pools of blood appear on your hands and arms, and wet air rushes in on you, and you want to whoop and shout, but you hear a noise, and you freeze.

He's come back. You stand there, not daring to move. Your legs tremble, your heart is going to leap right out of your chest. Minutes pass. Maybe hours.

You start talking to yourself, telling yourself it's okay, that every day he only comes back after dark. "Every day it's the same thing," you whisper to yourself. You tell yourself that's a fact, and you can depend on facts. Poppy says so. How many times have you heard him say, "Facts are what I want, not stories."

You take a deep breath and you don't whisper when you say, "He's not in the house, and he's not coming back until it's dark." You say it out loud, and you say it *loud*, so you can hear yourself. And you go to the window.

FRIDAY, 9:44 A.M.

YOU TURN THE pail over, try not to step in the pee that spills out, and put the pail upside down under the window. You step up onto it, and now you can really see out. The fresh rain splashes your face, and for a few moments it's enough just to be breathing the air. Below you is the steep metal roof, shiny in the rain, and below that a tangle of bushes and trees, and somewhere below them is the ground.

Shards of glass, jagged as teeth, are still stuck in the window frame. You're afraid to touch them. You wrap the blanket around your hand and loosen one piece after another. They fall to the roof and slide down, the way you're going to slide down. When you do that, when you slide down the roof and then jump to the ground, will you break your bones? Will you die?

That's when you think about not doing this, about staying in the room. You'll have to confess, but at least it's safe here. You can keep hoping that he'll let you go. He tells you he loves you. He feeds you. He's bringing you cookies tonight.

The wind blows across your face, and now the high, living buzz of the town comes to you, and you think of your family. Two crows fly overhead and call to you. They're saying your name. *Autumn, Autumn*, they shout hoarsely.

"I'm coming," you answer the crows. "I'm coming!"

FRIDAY, 9:56 A.M.

YOU THROW THE blanket across the window frame and climb up onto the sill. You crouch there for a moment, holding on to the window frame. Then you stick out your legs, close your eyes, and then you let go.

You go down so fast you almost fly off the roof. It's as if the roof's a living thing and it grabs you and flings you down its slick, wet, slippery surface. Your hands scrabble frantically to hold on to something, but there's nothing, you're just *going*, and when there's no more roof, the ground comes up to meet you. But instead of the ground stopping you, you're still falling.

You scream something—"what . . . wait . . ."—and your

mouth is full of dirt, and you're falling and tumbling and falling down a rocky slope. You come to a stop with your face buried in wet leaves. You lie there, breathing, and every breath you take hurts. But you're alive, and you're out. You're free.

FRIDAY, 10:16 A.M.

YOU CRAWL TO YOUR hands and knees. Every part of you aches. You wish you never had to move again. You listen. You hear wind. You hear water. You hear your own raspy breaths. You hear rustling noises, like soft footsteps. Is it him? Is he coming? You want to cover yourself in leaves and stay that way forever, but you get to your feet and look around. You're in a ravine with a creek winding through it. Poppy told you that if you're ever lost, stay by the water. You limp along next to the creek, holding your ribs. You crawl over fallen trees and stumble over rocks. Once, you fall and just lie there for a while, moaning. Then you get up and keep going.

After a while you hear road sounds above you, and you start pulling yourself back up the ravine. You go step by step, crawling and hanging onto trees and bushes.

When you get to the top, the road is right there, and you start walking. You just pick a direction and hobble along. It's still raining, and you're soaked. Your jeans and T-shirt are plastered to your body. When you hear a car in the distance, you crouch and roll into the bushes, curling yourself into a muddy ball and praying that if it's him in the car he won't see you, he won't hear your heart thudding. You know he's out there looking for you. You know he wants you back. He said he wants to keep you forever.

For a while there are no cars. The trees drip water, the wind blows, and something rustles in the underbrush. *Footsteps?* You choke back a scream just as a chipmunk scurries across the road in front of you. You walk again, shivering, your arms wrapped around yourself. Every time you hear the sound of a motor, you scuttle into the woods and hide and pray.

Somewhere you lose a sneaker, so you take the other one off and limp along, telling yourself that soon you'll find a house or see someone you can trust. A boy on a bicycle comes up on you. He's wearing a helmet and tight black cycling pants, and he's bent over the handlebars. He looks at you, cycles past, then swings around and comes back. "What's the matter with you?" he calls.

You turn and hobble the other way. "Hey," he calls, but you just keep going, and when you look again, he's no longer in sight. But now another car is coming, and you try to hide, but you're hurting and tired and not quick enough. The car stops.

A voice says, "Get in."

FRIDAY, 12:33 P.M.

"GET IN," THE woman behind the wheel says again.

You peer in the passenger side window at her. Is it a trick? What if she's a friend of the man?

"Where are you going?" she says. "I'll take you there. I'm on my way to Haverhill."

Haverhill? That's miles away from Mallory. You back away. You're shivering.

She leans over and opens the passenger door and exclaims,"My Lord, child! What happened to you? Get in this car right now. I'm not leaving you out here like this."

You look at her and remember how you followed the man into his house, and you don't budge.

"What?" she says. "You don't trust me? I have a daughter your age. Here—you want to see her picture?" She fumbles in her pocketbook on the seat next to her and pulls out her wallet. She flips it open and shows you a picture of a smiling girl.

You slide into the car, but you sit close to the door, ready to grab the handle, in case you have to get out fast.

"Where do you live?" the woman says.

You can't speak. You're so cold your teeth are chattering.

The woman turns on the heat in the car. "You don't have to tell me anything," she says. "Just nod yes and no. Do you live in Kent?" You shake your head. "Where I'm going, Haverhill?" You shake your head. "East Mallory? No? Mallory? Ah, that's it," she says, and she turns the car around.

FRIDAY, 1:03 P.M.

YOU OPEN THE front door and limp into the house. You look around like you can't believe everything is here, just the way you left it. You hear Mommy calling from the kitchen, "Hello? Is someone there?"

You say, "It's me, Mommy. Autumn."

You hear screams, and then Mommy comes running in, and behind her are your sisters and Poppy, and they're all saying your name.

TIMES STAR

Established 1899   Sunday morning edition

"I may not agree with what you say, but I'll defend to the death your right to say it."

MALLORY FAMILY REUNITED: QUESTIONS REMAIN

Mallory—On Friday the family of Blossom and Huddle Herbert of Mallory was reunited with their youngest daughter, Autumn Huddle, 11, who had been missing since last Sunday. She was returned to the family by Connie Rappaport, 46, of Haverhill. Rappaport was coming back from a visit to her grandmother, Arla Allen, who resides in the Five Birches Retirement Home in East Forge. Rappaport spotted Huddle walking on County Road at approximately 12:30 Friday afternoon and offered her a ride. "Poor little thing," Rappaport said, "she was all bent over and just soaked. I didn't realize at first that she was the child I read about in the newspaper. You don't expect to find her that way, you just don't, but when I took a good look at her, I knew."

The Huddle girl was examined at the Wertheimer Health Clinic on River Road and treated for cuts, bruises, and two broken ribs. Beauty Herbert, 17, said, "We felt in our hearts that Autumn would never run away, which some people were thinking, but we knew she wouldn't do that. We are so happy to have her back home." Blossom Herbert, the child's mother, also spoke to reporters and said, "I knew I would get her back, I never had a moment's doubt. I guess it's a mother's instincts."

Police are not answering questions about the cause of Autumn's disappearance. Mallory Police Chief Mark Cleveland said the matter is under investigation and police still want to talk further to Autumn and her family members. Anyone with information is asked to contact the Mallory Police Department (555-3166).

TIMES STAR

Established 1899   Monday morning edition

"I may not agree with what you say, but I'll defend to the death your right to say it."

MAN FALLS FROM WATER STREET RAILROAD BRIDGE

MALLORY—An unidentified man was seen falling from the Water Street Railroad Bridge on Saturday evening at approximately 6:10 P.M. Miss Heather Gardenia, 88, who lives in a third-floor apartment overlooking the bridge, called police to report seeing a man fall or jump into the North Branch of the Niskcogee River from the pedestrian walkway on the Water Street Railroad Bridge.

Miss Gardenia was watering her plants, which she keeps in the south-facing window, when she observed the man standing on the bridge. "I thought he was just enjoying the look of the water," she said. "I look at it all the time. It's raging with all that rain we've had." When she glanced up, she said, "not more than a minute later," according to her report to police, she observed the man pitching off the bridge and falling into the river.

Divers from the state police were in the water all day Sunday, but no body was recovered. "It's possible, but unlikely, that someone could survive that fall," Mallory Police Chief Mark Cleveland said. "If there is a body, it will turn up downstream at some point." The level of the Niskcogee is considerably higher than usual, due to the unusual amount of rain that has fallen this month. According to the weather station, April was the rainiest month in the past 40 years.

Mallory Town Manager William Defrost said the town would close access to the bridge walkway, which has been in need of repair for some time. He added that the mayor and town council would probably request that the state contribute to the cost, as the town does not have the necessary funds.

The man remains unidentified, and no one has been reported missing. Anyone with information is asked to contact the Mallory Police Department (555-3166).

PART FOUR

LAST REPORT FROM THE FAIRLY HAPPY HUDDLE FAMILY

SIT TIGHT

THE POLICE OFFICERS who show up at the house are Detective Brantley, who has a round, kind face, and Sergeant Gomez, who is round all over and impatient. All week they pick you and Beauty up at the end of the day and drive you around Mallory looking for the house. You find it on Thursday. It's on Woods Street, which isn't even on the city map.

"So this is the place? Are you sure?" Sergeant Gomez asks. You nod. You're all sitting in the patrol car, staring at the house. "Are you sure?" she says. She asks everything twice.

"Yes," you say. You're shivering. Of course you're sure.

Everything is just like you described it to them. The empty street, the waste fields on either side of the house, and the woods beyond the fields and behind the house. And the house, just like you said, is tall and narrow and unpainted.

"Okay. Sit tight, kid," Detective Brantley says. The two of them get out of the car and, just like on television, they have their hands on their guns, and they pound on the front door and yell, "Police! Open up!"

You sit in the car, and now your teeth are chattering. Beauty takes your hand, and that's good, but your teeth still chatter. If he's in there, will they shoot him? No, they'll take him prisoner and bring him out, and they'll put him right in this car. A rash breaks out all over your body. You're burning up. When he sees you, he'll go crazy, you know he will.

"Police! Open up!" they're yelling again. They try the door, but it's locked. They look in the windows, and up to the second floor, and then they come back to the car and Sergeant Gomez leans into the car and says, "I don't see any broken window."

"It's in . . . there," you say, pointing.

"Okay, let's check it out."

You and Beauty get out of the car, and you all walk around to the back of the house. "Oh my God," Beauty says. Up there is the gaping window and the metal roof you went flying off. And down there, just a few steps away, is the ravine you fell into, so deeply wooded you can't see to the bottom.

You all go around to the front of the building. "Get in the car," Detective Brantley says to you and Beauty. Then he and Sergeant Gomez use their clubs to break a window. They take out their guns and a flashlight and climb into the house and disappear.

The sun is going down, and you can't get rid of the thought that any moment now he's going to appear. "Lock the doors," you say to Beauty. You hear a noise, and your throat goes dry, and you slide down in the seat.

"It's okay, honey," Beauty says.

She's got her arm around you when they come out of the house. Just the two of them. Sergeant Gomez gets behind the wheel. "He's gone," Detective Brantley says as he stuffs himself into the patrol car. "Flew the coop," he says. "Not a sign."

You want to ask if they looked *everywhere*, in the closets and the bathroom, and under the bed. Maybe

Detective Brantley knows what you're thinking. He turns around to you and repeats, "Not a sign of him, Autumn. He's gone, clean as a whistle."

You say those words to yourself . . . *he's gone.* . . . You watch out the window until Sergeant Gomez turns the corner and you can't see the house anymore, and then you say those words to yourself again—*he's gone*—and, oh, how you want to believe them.

HISS LIKE A SNAKE

"JUST TAKE YOUR time making up your work, Autumn," Mr. Spiegleman says the day you go back to school. He's matter-of-fact and ordinary with you, but most everyone else sort of tiptoes around you, as if you've had a horrible sickness or something. Some kids don't talk to you at all, just stare at you as if they've never seen you before. This one girl, Bethany, comes right up to you and blurts, "You look normal," as if she expected to see you all deformed and hideous looking.

Your cuts and bruises are mostly healed up, but your ribs still hurt, especially at night. You're not sleeping that well anyway, waking up at every little noise, with your heart racing and your hands sweaty. You look sort of pale, and you're walking a little hunched over because of your ribs. Maybe that's why these three upper-grade boys who see you going into school one morning act scared of you.

The tall one with long hair hisses like a snake, and then they all make the snake sound, with their mouths tight and mean, and they put up their hands and say, "Keep away! Keep away from us." And they jump back, as if they don't dare let you even get near them. And then they laugh.

You pretend not to care and just walk on up the steps, but for the rest of the day you think about it. How they hissed. What they said. And how they knew who you were. Can everybody tell what happened, just by looking at you?

That night, after you're sure that Fancy is asleep, you climb up to Stevie's bunk and tell her about the snake sounds. She snorts and says, "Honestly, boys can be such jerks," and she pats your shoulder. "Just forget them," she advises.

She's so nice, and you like that, but the next day when you eat lunch with Mrs. Kalman, you're still thinking about the hissing and all the rest of it. After you tell her, she says, "How did it make you feel, Autumn?"

You answer that in one word: *weird*. She asks if you can

say anything else about it, and you shrug and take a drink of your soda. She goes on nibbling potato chips and waiting for you to speak, like she does. And finally, you say that word again. "It's just *weird* that people act as if I'm all different now, as if I'm not me anymore."

Mrs. Kalman nods and says, "I know that must be really frustrating to you."

"Yes!" you say. That's *it*. You wouldn't have thought to say that word, but she knows just how to put things.

"Maybe you should write about this in your journal," she says. "You know how helpful that is."

You shrug again, because you haven't written in the journal since, well, since *before*, and even though that's only a couple of weeks, it seems way longer, like maybe a year.

"So will you do that, Autumn?" Mrs. Kalman says, and you say, "Okay," and that night you try to do it, because you said you would, but all you write are two sentences.

Why do people treat me as if I'm all of a sudden someone else? I'm just the same person I always was.

After that you have nothing else to write, because the fact is—and you know this—you aren't the same as you were before you walked into that house. You're still Autumn Huddle, but you're definitely not the same. You've changed.

261

POSITIVE ID

SATURDAY THE DOORBELL rings. "Who is it?" you scream. *Has he come back . . . looking for you*? Your face flushes sickeningly hot.

Stevie goes to the door. You hover behind her. The two police officers are standing there. What are they doing here? You found the house, and it was empty, and the man was gone.

"We have some good news," Detective Brantley says. He takes off his cap and twirls it on his thumb. "We found out who owns the house, and we got some good information about our man."

Our man? You hate hearing that.

Then Mommy comes to the door and says, "What's going on here?"

"Hello, Mrs. Herbert," Detective Brantley says, "We think we have an ID on the man who kidnapped Autumn."

Mommy takes you by the shoulders and holds on to you.

"Mrs. Herbert," Sergeant Gomez says, "we need Autumn to look at some pictures. We're parked right over there, and we'll have her back in no time."

Mommy holds your shoulders even tighter, and she says, "I ain't letting her look at all those perverts. Anyway, if you know who he is, why do you need her?"

"We need Autumn to make the positive identification," Detective Brantley says. "She's the only one who can confirm the ID."

Mommy starts to object again, but you say, "Mommy, it's okay, I'll go."

"Not without me," Mommy says.

At the police station they sit you down at a table and Mommy sits right down next to you. Sergeant Gomez puts a notebook in front of you and says, "Look at the pictures and tell us if you recognize anybody. We don't say anything; it's all up to you. I'll turn the pages for you. You just give me the sign when you're ready."

You nod. Your hand is over your stomach, 'cause it's doing that clock ticking thing again.

"Take your time, Autumn," Detective Brantley says. "If you see a face you recognize, you tell us, but if you don't see anybody, that's okay. This is not a test or anything."

Sergeant Gomez opens the notebook, and you look at the faces on the first page and shake your head. She flips the page over. Mommy looks at you. You shake your head.

Sergeant Gomez turns the page. Look. Shake. Another page. Look. Shake. Another page, and another. Nobody says anything. Face after face after face, mostly men. What's weird is that a lot of the faces resemble his. You can't figure it out, and then you do. They're ordinary looking. They don't look like monsters or perverts. They don't look like bad people.

The pages turn, the faces blur, your stomach ticks. You're hating this. It's making you remember.

"Hello? Autumn, you still with us?" Sergeant Gomez says. She turns the page.

You look, you shake your head. Another page. No. Another. No. Another—*yes*.

You see him. No mustache, but that's him. You will never forget his face.

"There," you say, and you point.

CORKSCREW SMILES

ARE YOU OKAY, Autumn? How are you feeling? Are you sure you're okay? Everybody says it. First the questions and then the weird smile, sort of like a corkscrew twisting inside itself. Mrs. Kalman is the only one who never gives you that corkscrew smile. Stevie tells you it's a scared smile. "People are pissin' afraid of what you'll say."

Not Mrs. Kalman. She's told you she knows you've got things you need to unload. That's her word. "Whenever you're ready to unload, Autumn," she says. "I'm listening."

You've told her a little, but not much. Today is one of your lunch days together and you've been staring at her long, shining gold hair, sort of mesmerized. She's wearing her hair loose today, just tucked behind her ears.

"What are you thinking about?" she says.

"Your hair."

"Why my hair?"

You kind of wave your hands around, and you start to say, "Oh, just because," but she's looking at you and waiting, like she's been waiting for weeks now, and you know that eventually you're going to tell her all the things you haven't said yet. So you might as well tell her this bit.

"He liked my hair, and, you know." You stop. That's all you want to say right now. Next time maybe you won't say anything and maybe you'll say everything.

Maybe you'll tell her the whole thing, how you went up to him, thinking he was just another person, like one of your neighbors or one of Poppy's friends, and how he locked the door and slapped you, and how he tied your hands and put you in the room and made you sit on his lap and all the rest. All the stuff you haven't told. Maybe next time you'll tell her all that.

TELL US EVERYTHING

"AUTUMN. AUTUMN Herbert. Over here."
Krystal Langlois, who's the most popular girl in sixth grade
and who never paid any attention to you for a single
moment before this, is calling to you across the lunchroom. What does she want? You stand there for a
moment, holding your lunch bag, and then you shrug and
walk toward Krystal's table, and it seems as if the whole
lunchroom is watching.

There's no room on either bench for you. You shrug
again, ready to leave, but the other girls in Krystal's posse
squeeze together and make room for you. You sit down
and say, "What do you want?"

"Oh, *wooo*," one of the girls says, "the fifth grader is fresh!"

"Shut up, Stacey," Krystal says. She has beautiful black hair and perfect teeth, and she gives you a big smile, showing all of them. Every girl at the table is a year older than you. They all dress better than you, with earrings and cute jeans and their hair really nice.

You open your lunch bag and wonder what Stevie would say about these girls. *Bunch of snobby hypocrites. You're too good for them!*

Since you came back, all your sisters have been super nice to you, but Stevie has been the biggest surprise. It started at the health clinic Mommy and Poppy took you to the afternoon you came home. You were still in your cruddy clothes, but Stevie made you put on one of her sweaters, and the next day she told you it was yours to keep. "It looks cute on you," she said, "better than on me." And then last night, just when you were falling asleep, she leaned over from the top bunk and said, "Autumn? I really missed you. And I love you." Then she flopped back into her bed, and it was almost like a dream. Except it wasn't.

"How *are* you, Autumn?" Krystal says as you take out your sandwich. You nod and say what you say when people ask you that question, which they do all the time. "I'm good."

"Good," Krystal says. "*Glad* to hear that! Glad for *you*."

You take a bite out of your sandwich and hope they don't notice your rashy hands.

Blaze Flanagan, who's almost as beautiful as Krystal, leans across the table and says, "Okay, Autumn, tell." Her eyes get really big. "Tell us everything."

"What?" you say through a mouthful of bread and cheese.

"Whaaat?" someone mimics.

"*Tell*," Blaze repeats. "We want to hear all about it. Did he really—" She looks at the other girls, who are leaning in, and she almost smiles, and then she tries to look sad and serious. "You know," she says. "Did he, uh—what was it like? I mean, *really*?"

You get that choked-in-the-throat feeling, like you can't breathe and almost can't move. But you do move. You stand, pick up your lunch bag, and walk away. You hear them laughing, but you don't care about people like that anymore, the stupid things they're saying or thinking about you.

You go outside and sit down under a big old pine tree.

It's chilly, and you're not wearing a jacket, but you don't care about that, either. It's *nothing* to you, after the things you've done. You don't go back in, even after the second bell rings. You don't go in until you can breathe again, breathe without thinking that the next breath won't ever come.

YOU CAN'T STOP

SOME DAYS IN school are good, like the two days a week you have lunch with Mrs. Kalman and you talk about things. Some days are not so good, like the afternoon when Mr. Spiegleman is explaining some work to you, and he says something and touches your arm, and you jerk away and yell, "Don't touch me!"

Right away he's saying, "I'm sorry, Autumn, I shouldn't have done that," and he looks really sorry, and not the least bit as if he's mad at you for screaming at him, but even so you can't stop saying it.

Don't touch me.

Don't touch me.

Don't touch me.

YOU REMEMBER

"WHAT DID MR. Spiegleman do?" Mrs. Kalman says on Thursday when you eat lunch with her.

"Nothing," you say. "Nothing. It was my fault."

"Well, maybe," Mrs. Kalman says. "Want some more chips?" she asks.

You shake your head. The first week you were home, you ate and ate and ate, like you could never get full, but then one night you just stopped eating halfway through the meal. And since then you haven't wanted to eat a lot. You lost your big appetite, and you don't know why. You've always been, well, sturdy, but now there are almost no more places to pinch, like he pinched you, on your waist and your arms, and other places, too, like where you're growing breasts. He pinched you there, and it hurt.

Mrs. Kalman takes a sip of her soda and says, "Can you show me what Mr. Spiegleman did?" You nod, and you touch her arm. "He touched you," she says. "I see." She picks up her sandwich and takes another bite, so you do the same with yours. "Anything else?" she asks.

"It's stupid," you say.

"What is?"

"I'm stupid." You hunch your shoulders. "He said something, that's all."

She nods and says, "You want to tell me what he said?"

It comes out of you in a whisper, as if it's a big secret. "He said, 'What's that rash on your hands?'" You cover your face and laugh through your fingers, because it's *so stupid* to be upset about that. You just couldn't stand to hear it, and you don't know why.

"Well," Mrs. Kalman says, "let's have our cookies, and you think about it, okay?"

You love Mrs. Kalman. She never tries to rush you or make you say anything, or do anything like "get over it," or "forget about it," or "remember that you're safe now." You never have to tell Mrs. Kalman *anything*. Mommy and

Poppy say stuff, and they want to hug you and kiss you and hold you all the time, and you kind of want that, but you also kind of really *don't*, and when you tell them, they get all confused and it makes them feel bad, and then *you* feel bad, and it's just a big mess.

You reach for a cookie and check out all the red, bumpy things on your hands. Some bad rash. Itches a lot, too. Last night Mommy put that soothing, white calamine lotion all over your hands and your arms, and she gave you a soft old cotton sheet and—

The sheet.

Now you remember. You remember that *he* noticed your rash. You remember what *he* said. The same thing Mr. Spiegleman said. You remember that *he* brought you a sheet. You remember too much.

SIX MONTHS LATER: ROSES

OUTSIDE PATRICK THE Florist Beauty sniffed the display of roses, then unlocked her bike. She still worked her ten hours every week with Patrick, but she'd added another twenty-five hours at the KwikStop. Now that she was eighteen, she was paying her parents rent and saving the rest. She pushed off and rode into traffic. Ten minutes later, after valiantly biking up the hill to the school, she leaned on the handlebars and scanned the shoving, chattering crowd of kids for Autumn. Today she didn't bother looking for Ethan—he had track practice. He usually managed to show up once or twice a week to walk home with her and Autumn. Sweet of him—above and beyond.

Over the summer, when he'd been pumping gas at the KwikStop, they'd become friends—just that. Not the man of her dreams, but a really good friend. That was unexpected, as in *not planned for*. Speaking of which, her eighteenth birthday—that birthday at which *Le Plan* had been aimed for so many years—had come and gone, and here she was, still in Mallory. By choice, and not chafing about it, either.

Something had shifted in Beauty. *Le Plan* wasn't dead so much as revised: it wasn't so fanatically about escape now—that had come to seem sort of, well, juvenile—but more about getting her associate degree at Community College, getting herself really educated, and *then* finding out if she still wanted to leave Mallory. A little more open-ended. A little more about exploring. A little less about Beauty, and a little more about other people.

She spotted Autumn coming down the steps, but she didn't wave. She watched her progress, noticed who she did or didn't talk to, and if she appeared sad or upset. That was happening less and less, but even after six months Beauty found herself still anxious about the effects of the abuse on her little sister, still surprised about the changes in Autumn, but mostly still overwhelmingly grateful that she had come back to them.

BREMEN HERALD

Your Community Newspaper

"We print all the news that's fit to print and none of the gossip."

BODY DISCOVERED IN RIVER

BREMEN—The badly decomposed body of a white male was discovered on Sunday by two experienced Bremen sportsmen. Charles Skulko, 69, and his cousin Bradford Skulko, 58, were duck hunting Sunday afternoon in a marshy cove in the lower reaches of the Niskcogee River when they noticed what they at first thought was simply a pair of shoes someone had lost. Chuckling, the two men investigated and soon realized the shoes were on a body.

Charles Skulko then called the state police on his cell phone and directed them to the site of the discovery. "It was all bloated and swollen," Bradford Skulko told this reporter. "A pretty bad sight. I'm an EMS tech, and I don't exactly faint at the sight of blood or anything like that, but this made me pretty sick." Dr. Ronald Mantelier, the county coroner, said it appeared that the body had been in the water for at least several months. It is not known if foul play was involved. Dr. Mantelier said he would not speculate on the cause of death until his examination was complete. He did add that the body was in an advanced state of decomposition. "Pretty much more decomposed than any corpse I've had to deal with," he said.

WHAT YOU DID

FROM INSIDE THE big glass front door of the school, you see your sister Beauty standing up on the pedals as she bikes up the last bit of the hill. She's lost five pounds in the last two months. Big smile when she told you this. Two months is almost exactly the amount of time she's been biking up Barker Hill Road in order to walk you home every day after school. "So you're doing me the big favor," she tells you.

But you know who's doing who the favor. Mim reminded you that Beauty takes time off from work at the florist shop and has to make it up. Mim herself waits for Fancy, who takes forever to get ready, and walks her home. Sometimes Stevie comes along with you and Beauty, sometimes you all go together.

You run out the door and down the steps to meet her. "No more riding today," she says first thing, fanning her face. "I'm boiling." It should be cool here in the mountains—it's already the third of November—but the whole state has been smacked with a heat wave, and the leaves are falling like rain.

"That's okay," you say. Sometimes you hop on the handlebars and you have the thrilling ride down the hill, both of you laughing and shouting. Now you walk the bike, and Beauty asks if you had a good day. You shrug and say, "I don't know. I yelled at some people."

"Why'd you yell?" she says.

"They were being nosy about—you know."

"So they probably deserved to be yelled at."

"Maybe," you say. After you have one of these yelling explosions, which always take you by surprise, you wonder if you're just a terrible person. You've been trying so hard to be *mature*, like remembering the good things about yourself and keeping your temper and not being scared of things you don't have to be scared about, like noises at night and seeing a strange man walking on your block.

Later, turning the corner onto Carbon Street, you jump on the bike and, as you pedal through a drift of fallen leaves toward your house, you make a deal with yourself, which is something Mrs. Kalman taught you to do. And the deal is that from now on, it's okay for Beauty to walk you home one or maybe two days a week. The other days you walk alone. And if, on those days, you find your stomach in knots, the other part of the deal is to remind yourself of what you did and how you saved yourself and how good that is.

You used to think that, unlike your sisters, you were the only one with nothing special about you, nothing at all, but now it occurs to you that you're really lucky—you've got the best part of each of your sisters. When the man had you locked up, you got wicked mad (like passionate Stevie), you thought about things (like smart Mim), you made a plan (like careful Beauty), and then—like yourself!—you carried it out. And it wasn't easy, but you did it. You had to get back to your family, which you love so much (like love-bug Fancy), love more than anything in the world.

The maple tree in front of the house has turned red overnight. You lean Beauty's bike against the porch, pick up a leaf to give to Mommy, and go in, calling, "Mommy? It's me. I'm home."

FUNNY AND SAD AND SCARY, TOO

HELLO, EVERYBODY in my class and Mrs. Sokolow my teacher that I love. Hello, how are you today? I am good today, and today for share time I will tell you a story that Autumn my sister told me. It is such a good story, and nobody fall asleep while I'm telling, please!

This story is funny and sad and scary, too! But don't worry, it has a happy ending. See, there was this girl, who was like a princess, and one day she walked into this cave and guess what? A creature lived in it. You know what a creature is? It could be a person or it could be an animal. It could be a monster!

The princess didn't know the creature lived there, she

was just like, la, la, la, I guess I'll take a walk and look in this cave. And then the creature came out and she was sooo surprised, and the creature said, Hello, princess, you came to visit me. The princess said, No, I didn't. I think I'll go home now.

But the creature said, No you have to stay with me because I love you and I'm going to put you in the tower and keep you there. So he did.

Oh, and I almost forgot. The creature wore a tie and eyeglasses, which is the funny part of the story. Isn't that funny? A creature with a tie and eyeglasses! It made me laugh *sooo* much.

So the princess lived with the creature for a long time, and every night he came to visit her and tell her he loved her. And he touched her toes and her knees and her fingers and her belly button! Touching the belly button! That's another funny part of the story, right?

But the sad part is that the princess missed her mommy and daddy, the king and queen of the land. She cried so much and she missed them every day and every minute, and that's *sooo* sad, and when Autumn my sister told me this part of the story, I cried, too, but she didn't.

But next comes the good part of the story! One day the

princess *made up her mind*. Yes, she did! She was going to get out of the tower. So she just jumped right out! And ran home. And the king and queen gave her a million hugs and kisses and everybody was happy again. The end.

Thank you. Good-bye. I'll sit down now.